THERE WAS A KNOCK AT THE DOOR . . .

"I'll go," called Sheila. "I'm dressed."

From the bedroom I heard the voice of Detective Dolan. "I've been looking for you since three this morning, Miss Gallegan. Where's Puma?"

I tied up my robe and went into the living room. "Here."

"Cozy, aren't you?" The detective looked at Sheila and then at me. "I suppose you two are going to be each other's alibi."

"Alibi for what?" I asked.

He held up a jet pendant earring. "It's yours, isn't it, Miss Gallegan?"

Sheila stared at it for a long moment. "Yes," she whispered. "It's mine."

"Okay," I turned to Dolan, "quit playing games. Where'd you find it?"

Dolan looked hard at the slim red-haired girl. "In a closed dead hand. Einar Hansen was killed last night—murdered."

Sheila's lovely face went white. Suddenly I wondered where she'd been those hours before I picked her up.

night lady

William Campbell Gault

Adams Media
New York   London   Toronto   Sydney   New Delhi

Adams Media
An Imprint of Simon & Schuster, Inc.
57 Littlefield Street
Avon, Massachusetts 02322

For information about special discounts for bulk purchases, please contact Simon & Schuster Special Sales at 1-866-506-1949 or business@simonandschuster.com.

Manufactured in the United States of America

ISBN 978-1-4405-5794-1
ISBN 978-1-4405-3915-2 (ebook)

This work has been previously published in print format by:
Fawcett World Library, New York, NY.

ONE

THE THING you want to remember about wrestlers is that they are not always as virile as they look. It's a trade that appeal to the narcissist. And from self-admiration it's only a step to love of like for like.

And love of like for like can lead a man into something as socially respectable as Rotary or something as socially repugnant as homosexuality. A distressing number of those groaning, sweating monsters you see hamming it up in the ring have lace-edged spats and colorful silk underwear hanging in their lockers.

Muscles do not make the man, even when they impress the woman.

I was never a wrestling fan, so I had never heard of Adonis Devine. Even if I had heard of him, I wouldn't have believed it. Would you believe anybody could be named Adonis Devine?

That's the name he gave me when he dropped in at my office one overcast morning. He didn't look too bulky in his street clothes and his face was pure, clean, new-coin Greek. He was an extremely handsome man.

The current pitch with these freaks is pseudo-intelligence, and they enunciate their awkwardly pretentious speech clearly and painfully. I couldn't understand why I disliked him on sight; if I had been a woman, I would have gone over the desk, lusting for him.

He told me his manager was missing, a man named Duncan Guest.

"Did he take any loot with him?" I asked.

He frowned. "I don't quite comprehend you, Mr. Puma," he said.

"If he's missing," I pointed out, "it could follow that he'd have reason to be missing, wouldn't it? He wouldn't blow without tapping the till, would he?"

He continued to frown. He said nothing.

"Aren't you comprehending me?" I asked him.

He shook his head.

"Who handled the money?"

"I handled all the money. Duncan is . . . well, shall we say, unknowing about things commercial?"

"You can say it if you want to," I agreed, "though it's stilted and silly phraseology. I can still hear your adenoidal overtones, Mr. Devine; go back to your Cedar Rapids dialect."

He smiled softly. "You're being rude, aren't you? You're giving me an excuse to break your back."

"I'm not trying to be rude," I said patiently, "but a relationship between a private investigator and a client is a tricky one. In order for it to be successful, it requires an exceptional honesty. Shall we start over from where you came in?"

His smile didn't dim. "All right. I get into bad habits, being interviewed on TV. Duncan Guest is a bad manager but a good friend. He hasn't been seen around town for two days and I'm afraid something might have happened to him."

"Have you notified the police?"

He shook his head slowly.

"Why not?"

I thought he colored. He stared at the top of my desk.

I asked gently, "Does your relationship with Mr. Guest go beyond business?"

He took a deep breath and shook his head again. "I'm a man, Mr. Puma. *I'm all man.*"

"Oh?" I paused. "A recent victory?"

He paused, too. And then nodded. "After a long and expensive succession of fifty-minute hours. And if you should ever repeat that, I *would* break your back. I'm not joking."

"I wouldn't think of repeating it," I said. "But if we're going to get along, don't threaten me. I don't scare that easily."

His smile came back. "Mr. Leonard told me that. He's the man who recommended you."

"All right, then," I continued, "you're cured. How about Guest?"

"He has always been—more or less normal. I mean, he lived with me, understand, but he had plenty of dates with women and he didn't take them out just for their dialogue."

"He doesn't sound like an admirable character," I said. "Was he bleeding you?"

"Never," he said. "Believe me, Duncan always paid his own way. He used to bet on the matches."

"Now wait," I said, "who'd bet on wrestling matches? You're not going to tell me that some matches aren't fixed, are you?"

"Of course not," he said. "But to answer your first question, *fans* will bet on wrestling matches. There are fans, Mr. Puma, who will get very indignant if you suggest that the outcome of *any* match is prearranged."

"All right," I said. "I've seen their faces on TV. I'll accept that for the moment. Let's get back to Guest—he was living with you; he left. Did he take his clothes?"

Devine shook his head. "That's why I'm worried about him."

"But you didn't go to the police because . . . well, because of involved relationships they might investigate?"

"That's correct, Mr. Puma."

I leaned back in my chair and studied him.

He returned my stare.

I asked as politely as possible, "Do you think he left because you—were cured?"

Some slight color in his face again. "No. We were friends, good friends, beyond—anything like that."

"He's never left like this before without telling you where he was going?"

"Never."

I studied him some more.

After a minute of it, he said, "You don't believe half of what I'm telling you, do you?"

"I find it difficult to believe you would pay to have this Duncan Guest searched for. Why should you? What is he to you, now?"

"Look, when I first came out here, fresh out of college,

we roomed together. We starved together. I'd been a cow college fullback, and I tell you I was green. Working at Douglas as a lousy assembler and getting nowhere fast. Duncan dreamed up the wrestling bit, dreamed up my name, conned the promoters into giving me a break—"

"I thought he didn't have any business sense."

"He's got promotional sense. He hasn't got any money sense. He knows how to make it, but not how to save it. And he's a sucker for a certain type of women."

"What type?"

"The blasé, the cynical, the hard-to-get. They were a challenge to Duncan Guest."

I asked, "Do you have a picture of him?"

"Not with me. At home. I can get it to you in an hour."

I sat and thought.

"What's the matter?" he asked. "Don't you need the business?"

"I need it. And I need the respect of the Police Department or I don't stay in business long. My license is issued by the state but my success depends on local cooperation. Why don't you report Guest's disappearance to Missing Persons?"

"You know why. We discussed that." He stood up. "There are other investigators."

He was halfway to the door when I said, "I'll go with you to get the picture. By the way, what's your real name?"

He turned around. "Clarence Kutchenreuter. Why?"

I smiled. "Guest did give you a better one, didn't he? Though a wrestler named Clarence Kutchenreuter would be a refreshing change. Is that German?"

"Right. Good Iowa German. And look at me now."

"It's a strange business," I agreed. "I would have sworn you were Greek."

He drove his car to his apartment and I followed him in mine. His apartment was at the eastern end of the Strip, an expensive apartment, expensively furnished and decorated, with a view of the city. This wrestling dodge was obviously paying Mr. Kutchenreuter very well.

There he gave me two pictures of Duncan Guest. One was a portrait, head and shoulders, and the other was a snapshot taken at the beach, Muscle Beach.

Duncan Guest was a well-built man and handsome in

an arrogant and pugnacious way. With the pictures, Adonis gave me a list of places where Guest could be inquired about. One I recognized as a hang-out for the bulging bicep monsters and another as a haven for the lavender lads. He gave me some names and two hundred dollars.

I was not happy about the job. But in my trade, we don't get the clean jobs. Those go to the Police Department. The people who hire private men have reasons why they can't enjoy the free municipal service. Some of the reasons are never revealed but I try to learn as many of them as I can. For my still-conscious conscience, battered though it is.

At Harry's Harlequin Bar, the fat and swarthy man behind the mahogany shook his head when I inquired about Duncan Guest. "Haven't seen Dunk in three days," he told me. "Who's looking for him?"

"I am."

He studied my card. "It says here 'Joseph Puma—Investigations, Credit Reports.' Something wrong with Dunk's credit?"

"Not that I know of."

"So you're working for somebody who misses him. Would the guy be blond and lavender?"

"He could be blond. What disturbs you about that?"

"I figured it for Adonis."

"So what?"

"Adonis is no friend of mine. I wouldn't help him find a collar button. He ain't been in here for a month."

"And your friends have to be customers, eh? Maybe Adonis has given up joints like this."

"What did you mean by that crack, mister? What did you mean by joints like this?"

"We both know," I said. "Let's not quibble."

He put his hands on the bar and stared at me. "I used to wrestle a little. I could throw you right through that window there with no trouble at all."

I shook my head. "And don't try it. Live in your memories, lard-butt. They're safe and soft and kind. Well, maybe you'll be more polite to the police when they ask you about Guest."

He nodded toward the booth. "There's the phone—call 'em."

I didn't bite. This was Santa Monica and I was not in good standing at the S.M.P.D. I said, "I don't have to. My client will."

He laughed. "Adonis? They know all about *him*. A lot of co-operation he'll get from the Santa Monica Department."

I shrugged. I said genially, "Good-bye, Harry Harlequin. Watch your weight and your tongue and you'll be all right." I left him glaring.

Muscle Beach wasn't far; I drove over there. The sun had broken through the overcast and the freaks were gamboling on the sand. Ugly with bunched muscle, tanned to a golden brown, they frolicked and postured, self-conscious and arrogant.

The sight of them was disturbing enough. But it was the pulchritude of their audience that bothered me most. Lovely and shapely girls in tight, brief swimsuits sat on the sidelines and simpered. How could they admire these monsters?

The thin, freckled man behind the counter of the hamburger stand seemed glad to see a man in street clothes. "What'll it be?" he asked with a smile.

"A couple cheeseburgers and some coffee." I took a stool and looked out at the kelp-strewn beach. "Not many here, are there? I suppose the sun will bring them out this afternoon."

He slid two pats of meat onto the griddle. "Not at this end of the beach. The solid citizens stay away from here. Just the muscle-men and their fans hang around here."

"How about Adonis Devine?" I asked. "Does he hang around here?"

"Not lately. You a fan of his?"

"Not exactly," I answered. "What sort of a fellow is he?"

The freckled man frowned and went to the refrigerator for two slices of cheese. "I don't know—" He shrugged. "Don't get me wrong, some of those mammoths out there are okay—solid citizens in a nice fat racket. And I always liked Devine. It's just—you know, a guy gets sick of looking at the same thing all the time."

"I know. How about a man named Duncan Guest? Ever hear of him?"

The man flipped the pats of meat over and put the cheese on the cooked side. "Hell, yes. Dunk and I play chess right there on the counter real often. He's okay, that Dunk. Once in a while I get a feeling he's double-gaited, but I don't think of it any more than I can help."

"Double-gaited?"

He turned to study me. "Am I talking Greek?"

I shrugged. "I'm one of those big virile wops. I don't know much about the weirdies."

He sliced two rolls. "I meant Duncan gets along with the boys *and* the girls. He had a girl in here the other night that made you weak just to look at her. And class, I mean real class, Beverly Hills class."

"Oh?" I paused. "Nothing personal, I mean—you've got a nice spot here, but it's not classy, right?"

He smiled. He put my cheeseburgers together and slid them onto a plate. "Right. And you wonder why Dunk would bring a Beverly Hills broad here?"

"Well, yes—"

He added sliced pickles and potato chips to the plate. "Dunk and I are good friends, real good friends."

"You knew he was living with Adonis Devine, didn't you?"

The freckled man looked at me steadily. "I knew that. Lots of guys live together and there's nothing wrong with it. Dunk brought the girl here to introduce her to his good friend."

"So all right already," I said. "You don't have to get hot about it."

"Okay," he said. "*Okay.*" He put the food in front of me and went to get the coffee. He paused and turned back. "What did you mean he *was* living with Devine? Isn't he any more?"

"Not for a couple of days. Devine hired me to look for him."

The man stared at me. "Dunk's missing? Matter of fact, he hasn't been around since night before last, at that."

"That would be Tuesday night," I said. "Devine hasn't seen him since Tuesday morning."

"He didn't come home Tuesday night?"

"Evidently not."

The man brought my coffee and stood staring out at the sea. Finally, he turned to face me. "I know about a place Dunk's got, a little apartment over a garage near here."

"A place of his own?"

"That's right. He used to use it when he had a broad on the line. I've used it myself a couple times. He didn't want to take any broads to Devine's place. I never let myself wonder why."

"Give me the address," I said.

"I'll do better than that," he told me. "I've got a key, too. But don't use it until you ring the bell for a long time, huh? He might be shacked up."

"I'll be discreet," I promised. "What kind of car does he drive?"

"A gray Austin Healey. You figure if you see the car, he should be there, huh?"

"In this town," I said, "natch."

It was a four-car garage, bleached and weather-stained stucco, bordering the beach in Venice. I looked through a small and grimy window and saw the Austin Healey parked at the far end. The three stalls between it and the window were vacant.

On the side of the garage next to the wooden, out-side stairs there were three names, none of them Dun-can Guest. The names were the occupants of apartments one, two and three. I went up the stairs and along the open wooden runway to apartment four.

I rang the bell and heard no stirring from within.

I rang it again, and the door to apartment three opened and a slim girl with reddish-blonde hair came out with a shopping basket.

I asked, "Does Duncan Guest live here?"

She nodded. "I don't think he's home, though. I haven't heard a sound from that place since Tuesday night. Dunk—I mean, Mr. Guest doesn't stay there all the time."

"I know," I said. "But his car is downstairs in the garage."

She stared at me, frowning. She shrugged and went

along the runway. She went around the corner and I heard her footsteps going down the stairs.

I waited for a few minutes after that before using the key Freckles had given me to unlock the door.

The apartment consisted of a living room, a kitchenette-dinette combination and a bathroom. Duncan Guest was in the bathroom.

He was on the floor in there, staring at the ceiling. He wasn't seeing anything. His throat had been effectively sliced. There was a razor blade on the floor near one outstretched hand.

TWO

IN A HOT and airless room of the Venice Station of the Los Angeles Police Department, Sergeant Macrae glowered at me across a desk. He was a tall, thin man with a sour Scotch face and he glowered well.

"So the man didn't answer and you opened the door. How?"

"With a key given to me by the proprietor of a hamburger stand at Muscle Beach."

"All right. Why?"

"Why did I open the door? Well, Guest's car was down in the garage. His business associate was worried about him. He was missing. Isn't it logical I'd open the door?"

"It might be logical, but it sure as hell wasn't legal."

"Oh yes it was, Sergeant. I was given the key by a man who had permission to use the apartment. By giving me the key, he also gave me permission."

Macrae was silent a moment, glaring at me.

"You know I'm right," I said.

"Permission to use the apartment for what, Puma?"

"I have no idea," I said. "You'd have to ask him. I just wanted to go in and look around."

"And how about this Greek?"

"What Greek?"

"The wrestler, Adonis. Why didn't he take his business to Missing Persons?"

"You'd have to ask him. He's not Greek; he's German." I lighted a cigarette. "His real name is Clarence Kutchenreuter."

"Don't try to be funny, Puma."

I said evenly, "I'm not, Sergeant. He might be, but I'm not. He told me that was his maiden name."

Macrae snorted. "Freaks. Ugly slobs."

"Not Kutchenreuter," I protested. "He's handsome."

Macrae leaned back in his chair and looked at me coldly. "I told you not to be funny. Maybe you could sit for a while and consider your sins. Maybe we ought to hold you for a while until life looks a little more serious to you."

"Maybe," I said. "I don't personally give a damn, Sergeant. I find a body, so I immediately phone you people. I guess I don't need to tell you there are private investigators in this town who would take off for a weekend in Palm Springs if they found a body. Cooperation, that's my guiding principle. You could phone Captain Bixby down at Headquarters if you want the word on that."

He stared at me for seconds and then picked up the phone on his desk. "Get me Captain Bixby at Central."

I smoked my cigarette and considered my sins while he waited for the connection to be completed. I thought of Freckles in the hamburger stand and of Adonis Devine. And then, for some reason, I thought of the redhead with the shopping basket.

She'd said "Dunk" before she'd corrected it to "Mr. Guest." She had been an attractive girl.

Captain Bixby must have told Sergeant Macrae what a fine fellow I was, because the sergeant didn't glare quite as fiercely after he replaced the phone in its cradle.

"What about this joint in Santa Monica," he asked me, "this pansy bed?"

'I don't know much about it," I told him. "I—don't get along so well with the Santa Monica Department."

"Who does? Is the proprietor a fat, greasy man?"

"That's right. He offered to throw me through his front window. I have a feeling he doesn't like my client."

"Any indication why not?"

"So far as I could figure it was because Adonis doesn't
trade there. I got the impression that Harry only likes
people he makes money off."

Macrae was silent, staring at his desk.

I asked softly, "Am I forbidden to investigate any
more? Some of the stations don't mind if I work along
with them."

"What's there for you to investigate?" he asked. "You
were hired to find this Guest and you found him. Were
you hired to do something else?"

"No, but I might be. He and Adonis Devine were not
only business associates, they were personal friends.
Adonis might want me to work on the murder."

"Why? With all the men we have, *competent* men,
why would he want you messing around in it?"

"People are funny, Sergeant," I answered. " Okay,
you've said 'no.'" I stood up. "I'll keep my nose clean."

"Sit down," he said. "I didn't say you could go."

I sat down.

He laid his index finger against his nose and stared
beyond me. "Captain Bixby expressed a high degree of
admiration for you."

I yawned.

"We're understaffed and overworked," he said. "This
is the biggest city in area in the United States. And we
simply can't cover it."

"I know it," I agreed. "And the taxpayers won't stand
for another raise. They've had too many in the last few
years."

He looked at me coldly.

"I've heard it all before, Sergeant," I explained. "From
men in the Hollywood Station and the West Side Station and from downtown. I was merely repeating what
I heard."

"What about this girl Guest was with Tuesday night?"
he said. "Did the hamburger man tell you her name?"

"No. I didn't ask him. It didn't seem important at the
time. But he said Guest introduced him to the girl so he
might remember it."

"It didn't seem important at the time? She was probably the last person to see Guest alive. She could easily
be the murderer."

"You've established it as murder?" I asked.

He stared at me. "What else?"

"I've no way of knowing," I said, "lacking your laboratory facilities. I saw the razor blade near his hand and considered it might be suicide."

Sergeant Macrae tapped the papers on his desk. "It was murder and it happened Tuesday night. Or call it Wednesday morning if you want. Between midnight and two o'clock."

I crushed my cigarette in the ashtray on the desk. I said nothing.

"Why would I be crowding you if I thought it was suicide?"

I shrugged. "Official venom. I run into it quite often."

He studied me coldly. "I'm surprised your face isn't marked more than it is. You must have been hit plenty of times."

"I weigh two-seventeen," I said. "That eliminates a lot of angry men, the small and medium-sized ones." I stood up once more. "Am I free to go?"

He nodded. "Keep in touch with us." He paused. "If you're hired to work on the case, phone me and we'll talk about it."

"All right, Sergeant. And thank you. If we do work together, I can guarantee you you'll have no reason to regret it."

"Don't wave the flag," he said. "Just stay on the right side of the fence and keep a civil tongue in your head."

"Yes, sir," I said. "Good-bye."

I didn't go back to the beach or to the garage apartments. I drove directly to the Hollywood Strip. I didn't know if Adonis was home or if news of Guest's death had been made public, but he hired me to find him and a report was due.

He opened the door to his luxurious dump and said. "Come in. News already?"

I came in and closed the door behind me. I said, "I found Mr. Guest. I found him dead. He was murdered."

It was the damnedest thing. He stood there, all man and muscle a yard wide, with that Greek god's face rigid in shock. He stared at me for uncomfortable seconds, and then he began to blubber like a baby.

I went to the window and looked out at the bright city.

Later, I warmed some milk in the kitchen and brought him a cup. He was relaxing on a white leather couch.

"Tell me about it," he said weakly. "Tell me how you happened to find him, everything."

I gave it to him play by play.

When I'd finished, he said, "Some day, I'm going to drop in on Harry. He's a malicious man." He clenched and unclenched his hands. "Who was the girl? What is her name?"

"I don't know. The police are probably working very hard to learn that about now. I guess Mr. Guest thought a lot of her. He took her down to meet that friend of his, the freckle-faced gent in the hamburger stand."

Devine's face stiffened. He said nothing.

I asked, "Did you know that Mr. Guest had this other apartment?"

He shook his head. "Or I would have told you. It would have been a logical place to look for him."

"Well," I said, "I only used part of one day. You have a refund coming."

"Keep it," he said. "I may phone you in a day or so. I know some things the police might not about Duncan's friends."

"If you do," I told him, "you had better tell the police right now. That's your duty as a citizen and as a friend of Duncan Guest's."

"I'll see," he said irritably. "I'll see. I'll phone you, Mr. Puma."

I went out quietly.

It was after five o'clock now and traffic on Sunset was murderous. I had two hundred dollars; I walked over to Creighton's for dinner. At Creighton's, you can get a pretty fair steak for seven dollars and I had one. I owed it to myself after the indignities of this day.

From there, I went to the office to type up my short report. That was a practice of mine that kept me on the right side of the Police Department. I made complete and honest reports of all cases and kept them available to the Department.

I picked up a paper on the way to the office, tomorrow's edition of the *Times*. The story was there, more of the story than I had known when I left Sergeant Macrae.

The police were looking for a woman. The redhead next door, the one I'd met with the shopping basket, had informed the police that there had been a ruckus in Mr. Guest's apartment around the time he had been killed. Then she had heard a scream and a thump, and had started to go to the phone to call the police.

She was just picking up the phone when she heard the door of Mr. Guest's apartment close. She had gone to her front window that looked out on the runway and seen a woman hurrying past toward the stairs. The woman had worn a white sheath dress and a cerulean mink stole (whatever that is, I thought). There had not been a sound from Guest's apartment since.

Further, the redhead had stated, though she had never met Duncan Guest, she was aware that he used the apartment infrequently and assumed he really lived somewhere else.

That was enough for the paper to dub this a "love-nest slaying" and enough for me to doubt the redhead. Because she had first called him "Dunk" when she'd talked to me, and now she had never met him.

The redhead's name was Sheila Gallegan and I put it in my little book.

The freckle-faced proprietor of the hamburger stand was quoted as explaining Duncan Guest had used the beach hideaway *solely* for the purpose of dreaming up new promotional schemes for his clients, all of whom were wrestlers.

Now there was a real friend. I put his name in the book under Sheila Gallegan's. His name was Einar Hansen.

The police laboratory had come up with the information that Duncan Guest had undoubtedly been hit with a bronze ashtray, staggered to the bathroom and collapsed and there had his throat sliced.

The client who had hired the prominent local Hawk-shaw, Joe Puma, was identified as Adonis Devine, but Mr. Devine had not been available for press interrogation.

The by-lined writer of all this new information has implied delicately that Mr. Guest was a notorious wolf

and possibly had been killed by an innocent repelling
his lustful advances.

How the innocent could be innocent enough to be led
to the apartment was not explained. Nor the conflicting
fact that an innocent wouldn't be likely to slice a man's
throat *after* he was unconscious and momentarily lust-
less.

One thing the writer had not learned was the real
name of Adonis Devine. I was one up on him there.

I was filing my report when my phone rang. It was
now nine o'clock and there would be no reason for a
client to assume I was in the office.

It was Greg Harvest, an attorney who got a lot of the
carriage trade and who now and then condescended to
throw me a bone.

He had a client, he told me, who had been out with
Duncan Guest the night he was murdered. Her name
was Deborah Huntington. She had seen my name in the
paper and she wanted to talk with me.

"When and where?" I asked.

"At her house. She and her brother are waiting for
you there. Do you know who the Huntingtons are?"

"Millionaires, aren't they?"

"I didn't mean that," Harvest said stiffly. "I meant it's
an old and highly respected family in this town."

"But also rich," I added, "or you wouldn't care how
old and highly respected they were."

"Stop the adolescent sniping, Joe. Don't you want the
business?"

"Yes, *sir*," I said. "Is there going to be business?"

"I'm—not sure. Her brother thinks I would be enough
protection against the law, but Miss Huntington thinks
otherwise. In any event, they'll pay you for your time
tonight, even if they don't hire you."

"Protection against the law? Elucidate, Greg."

"Haven't you read the paper? A woman was with this
Duncan Guest when he was killed. That was a couple
of hours after Miss Huntington left him, but are the
police going to think so? The maid will testify that
Miss Huntington came home that night at eleven-thirty,
but the police have a middle-class notion that servants
can be bought."

"I see. So Miss Huntington might want to hire me to investigate the murder?"

"She might."

"What about her papa? Would he agree?"

"The senior Huntington died a year ago, Joe, and her mother two years before that. The estate was split evenly between Miss Deborah and Mr. Curtis Huntington."

"Curt Huntington—" I said. "That gent who owns the Wilshire Arena?"

"That's one of the Huntington properties, yes."

"Is that how Deborah met Duncan—through the wrestling at the Wilshire Arena?"

"I have no idea. Joe, you're interrupting a bridge game. Why don't you ask the Huntingtons these questions?"

"Okay," I said sadly. "Greg, I knew you when you played pinochle. You've certainly come up in the world."

He didn't comment on that. He gave me the address of the Huntingtons and hung up without a good-bye.

The address was a Beverly Hills address. Beverly Hills, like Santa Monica, is a distinct and separate municipality with a police department of its own. I got along with the Beverly Hills Department very well. I had worked there for four years.

It was late and my beard stubble was showing. I shaved in the office before driving to the Huntingtons'.

It was a fieldstone house on a summit overlooking the Dade Country Club. It was sheltered from the road by Lombardy poplars.

The maid told me the Huntingtons were expecting me and led me to a lofty, paneled room that ran the length of the pool in the rear of the house.

Curtis Huntington stood near a leather-upholstered bar; a dark, slim and attractive girl sat in a chair nearby. I recognized the girl as one I had seen in a few recent TV dramas.

Curtis Huntington was one of those slim and elegant men who wear clothes as though they invented them. He introduced me to his sister.

I smiled at her and said, "We have a mutual friend. Einar Hansen."

She smiled back as her brother frowned. She looked

at him and explained, "That man in the hamburger stand. He's—I mean, he *was* a very good friend of Dunk's."

Huntington nodded toward a soft leather love seat and I sat down. He said, "My sister thinks it would be wise for you to investigate the death of Mr. Guest."

"Don't you, sir?" I asked him.

He said thoughtfully, "I'm not sure. The police are going to learn Deborah was out with him that evening. But we have a number of witnesses who will swear she was home at eleven-thirty."

"A number? I thought there was only a maid to testify."

He shook his head. "A maid and a housekeeper and a neighbor. The neighbor came over, as a matter of fact, to borrow some seltzer for a party they were giving and talked with Deborah."

"In that case," I admitted, "you don't really need me."

Deborah said quietly, "Maybe I do. I'd like to know about Duncan Guest and I can afford to pay for the information."

I studied her. She looked at me candidly and without any apparent grief.

Her brother said, "Duncan was a very good friend of ours. Despite his . . . background, he had all the instincts of a gentleman."

A *double-gaited gentleman,* I thought, but didn't voice it. I said, "Because of his . . . background, I'd be interested in learning where you met him, Miss Curtis."

"At a party," she said, "in Hollywood." She smiled. "I was introduced to him by Luscious Louis. Have you heard of Luscious Louis?"

"A cheap imitator of Gorgeous George," I said lightly, "and a lousy wrestler to boot."

Curtis Huntington wrinkled his nose and said nothing.

I asked, "And how did you meet Luscious Louis, Miss Huntington? Understand, I'm not investigating *you,* but frankly he doesn't seem like the kind of man who would move in your circles. Did you meet him through your ownership of the Wilshire Arena?"

She shook her head. "I met Louis through my agent and the rest of them through Dunk—Mr. Guest. They're really much more interesting personalities than you'd imagine from their ring performances."

"That wouldn't be hard," I said. "Slumming, really then, weren't you, Miss Huntington?"

She colored faintly and her chin lifted. "I had no such thought in mind," she said stiffly, "and I am beginning to doubt the advisability of hiring you."

I stood up. "Why don't you sleep on it? There's been a disturbing lack of honesty here tonight." I turned toward the door.

Deborah Huntington said, "One moment, Mr. Puma. You haven't been dismissed."

I turned to stare at her. "Dismissed—? I'm not a servant, Miss Huntington. I have my own business and the right to pick my own clients."

She took a deep breath. "I'm sorry. That was a bad choice of words. But I—had a feeling you personally dislike me."

"I don't even know you, Miss Huntington. But you've shown me a familiar pattern tonight: the beautiful daughter of a respected family getting involved with trash."

Curtis Huntington protested, "Duncan Guest was far from trash, Mr. Puma. You obviously never knew him."

I faced him. "That's right. The first time I met him, he was dead. I was speaking of his friends."

"Einar Hansen was a friend of his," Deborah Huntington said. "Do you consider him trash?"

"Not so far as I know him. But he's certainly not a man who would normally move in the Huntington coterie, is he?"

Deborah Huntington stared at me. "My God, you're a snob! A man in your trade a snob—it's incredible."

"I'm not a snob," I answered. "But I am always leary of people who try too hard to prove that they aren't."

She glared. Her brother chuckled and said, "Why don't we all have a drink? Somehow, we got off on the wrong foot."

She ignored him, her dark eyes glinting angrily. And then her lovely face softened and she half smiled. She said, "He might be right. Let's call a temporary truce."

I shrugged. "Okay, if it's good booze."

Her brother said, "I have any kind you want. Good booze for my friends and cheap booze for Deborah's."

"Consider me one of your friends," I told him, "just for tonight."

It was Jack Daniels and how often did I get a chance to drink that? He poured me a mammoth slug of it and added ice and a minimum of good mountain water. We sat and talked.

The picture of Duncan Guest that emerged from this conversation was radically changed from the picture I had in my mind after talking with Adonis. But then, Einar Hansen had changed it, too, and I had learned long before tonight that one can learn very little about a man from hearsay alone. Guest could easily have been different from all his friends' appraisals.

I had enough Jack Daniels to mellow me, and we were almost friends by the time I left. Deborah wanted to hire me before that, but I repeated that it would be best if she withheld her decision until tomorrow.

First of all, I wanted to be sure she had come home at eleven-thirty on Tuesday night.

And stayed home.

THREE

ADONIS DEVINE received a nice promotional splash in the next day's papers. He had offered a reward of three thousand dollars for information leading to the arrest and conviction of Duncan Guest's murderer.

In the story, Guest was identified as Duncan's manager and publicity man but not as his roommate. At one time, early in their respective careers, according to Adonis, Guest had divided his last dollar with him.

It was a properly sentimental account and there was a pose of Adonis in wrestling tights, arms crossed, feet spread and handsome face aglow in anticipation.

The boy from Iowa had learned about promotion.

I phoned Sergeant Macrae before going down to the office. I told him Miss Huntington wanted to employ me and I wondered if she had been cleared.

"She's been checked," he said. "Unless she's got two lying servants and a lying neighbor, she's clear. We're checking them now."

"Which brings us back to Joe Puma," I said. "What's your decision on me, Sergeant?"

"I don't make those decisions," he said. "I talked it over with Captain Michaels and he said it would be all right, if you kept in daily touch with us."

"Fair enough, Sergeant. Thank you. How about the Syndicate? Are you checking into that?"

"What Syndicate?"

"The wrestling syndicate, Sergeant. Somebody from on high has to decide who wins which bouts, doesn't he?"

A silence, and then, "Are you trying to be funny again, Puma?"

"Believe me, I'm not. It's a big business and it's staged. Now, there has to be *someone* who decides, doesn't there?"

"Sure," he said, "and that would be a job for you. You dig into that, Puma. And keep me posted." He hung up.

At my office, the phone-answering service informed me that a Miss Huntington had called and was expecting a return call. I opened my mail, first, and was rewarded by a check only six months overdue. Things were picking up.

Deborah Huntington asked, "Well, Mr. Puma?"

"I'm agreeable if you are," I answered. "There's a contract that has to be signed. Shall I bring it out?"

"If that's your usual service. I wouldn't want to impose. After all, you're not a servant."

"At a hundred a day and expenses," I assured her, "I'll be your servant while it lasts."

"Never mind," she said. "I'm leaving now anyway. Couldn't you mail it to me? Or I'll be shopping—I could drop in at your office."

"I'll mail it to you," I told her. "I don't spend much time in the office."

The bank was open by now; I took the check over there before going up to the Strip.

Adonis was in a dressing gown when he opened the door to me. He said, "I've decided to let the reward be the incentive, Mr. Puma. I won't be hiring you on a daily basis."

"I already have a client," I said. "I came for information, not your business."

He stared at me. Then, "Come in."

I came in and he nodded toward an electric percolator on the coffee table. "I'm just having coffee. Would you like a cup?"

"I would, thanks." I went over to sit on a davenport. "What about this Einar Hansen? Do you know him very well?"

"We were never close friends. I know him pretty well. He's certainly no killer. It was a girl who killed Duncan, anyway, wasn't it?"

"It seems logical to guess that, if the story of that girl next door can be believed."

Devine poured me a cup of coffee. "You got any reason to doubt her?"

"Some. I wasn't really thinking of Hansen as the murderer. But he was such a good friend of Duncan Guest's, I thought there was a possibility he knew more about him than he told the police."

Devine said quietly, "I didn't know he was such a good friend. Duncan certainly didn't talk about him much."

I didn't argue with him, I sipped my coffee and asked, "Do you have any favorite suspects?"

He frowned and stared at the carpeted floor. "I—would hate to say anything that would jeopardize my career." He looked at me. "Or my neck."

"I'm a *private* investigator," I reminded him.

He took a deep breath and looked past me. "I don't know who the big boys are in this . . . game. But I know who the policeman is. Through him, you might get to the big boys."

"The policeman—?"

"That's right. Mike Petalious."

"I'm not following you," I said. "What do you mean by *policeman?*"

"The man who keeps the boys in line. Every once in a while, you see, some wrestler might decide he could do it honestly, wrestle his way to prominence in honest matches. Well, there are a couple of ways that can be stopped. After his first straight bout, he wouldn't get another. But what if he beefs, threatens to get political about it, go to the boxing and wrestling commission?"

"You tell me."

Devine shrugged. "He's matched with Petalious. Now, most of the hams you see on TV couldn't honestly defeat their mothers. But Petalious is a wrestler, and a real nasty one. He can cripple you. He can send you into another trade."

"I see," I said. "The policeman, Mike Petalious." I put his name in the book. "But that wouldn't have anything to do with Duncan Guest, would it? He never wrestled."

"No, he didn't. But he had a real weird idea. He thought that honest wrestling would pay. I mean, just for the change." Adonis shook his head sadly.

"You don't think it would pay?"

Adonis looked at me wonderingly. "You're kidding. You've got to be. Have you ever seen it?"

I shook my head.

"I wrestled some in college," he told me. "It's real dull. You take about twenty minutes to find a hold on a man and he takes a half hour to try to wriggle out of it. Dullest damned sport in the world. You couldn't get two dozen people in this town to watch it."

"So, okay," I said. "And you think Duncan tried to find out who the big boys are so he could suggest this world-shaking idea of his?"

"I know he did."

I finished my coffee. I asked, "Do you think Curtis Huntington could be one of the big boys?"

"Do you mean the man who owns the Wilshire Arena?"

"That's the man."

Adonis shook his head. "Huntington's not really interested in wrestling. As a matter of fact, he thought so little of it he was encouraging Duncan to put his idea over, just for fun."

"Maybe," I said, "Duncan Guest was killed after he talked with Mike Petalious. Maybe the big boys don't like people who try to find out about them."

"It's a possibility," Adonis said grudgingly. "I'll stick with the woman theory. Duncan was quite a wolf." He paused. "Among both sexes."

"Do you have Petalious' address?" I asked. "Or could I find it in the phone book?"

"I don't have it. It could be in the book. Who's your client, Mr. Puma?"

"A lawyer by the name of Gregory Harvest. I get quite a lot of work out of him."

"And what's his interest in Duncan's death?"

"I don't know. Where's your phone book?"

There was a Mike Petalious in the phone book with a Brentwood address. He was the only man of that name in the Western Section Phone Book, and Adonis was certain he was the man known as the "policeman."

At the doorway, Adonis said, "Call on me any time. I'll be glad to help all I can."

"Just keep that three thousand dollars posted," I told him. "That's the biggest help of all."

I could be wasting my time. There was a very strong possibility that the death of Duncan Guest was in no way connected with the wrestling dodge. The fact that he had probably been killed by a woman would seem to indicate that his extracurricular tomcatting had led to his death.

But if he was a man of many conquests, which currently seemed likely, delving into the backgrounds of his many conquests would take more time than most of us are allotted on this earth.

The kind of women he must have known weren't generally ready to die or kill for love. He could have been killed by a woman, but not because of love. Or even lust.

- The address of Mike Petalious was the rear half of a modest stucco duplex on Braham Street. The joint was saved from complete banality by the stark white of the stucco against the rich red of the bougainvillaea that climbed all over it.

A woman in shorts and halter was in front of the Petalious address, adding peat moss to a window box that fronted the picture window.

She was no midget. I would guess that she weighed in just under the middleweight limit of a hundred and sixty pounds. But she was tall and nowhere pudgy. She was an extremely seductive big woman.

She turned to smile at me as I came up the walk. Her hair was black and lustrous, her smile warm.

"I'm looking for Mike Petalious," I told her.

"He should be here any minute," she said. "Do you want to wait out here or in the house?"

"This will do. Are you Mrs. Petalious?"

She smiled. "What makes that your business? I could be, some day."

I smiled back at her. "Sorry. My name is Joe Puma. I'm investigating the death of Duncan Guest."

"For Adonis?"

I shook my head. "Why did you ask that?"

"Because if you were working for Adonis, this would be the first place he'd send you. Mike put him out of business for three months."

"Really? How?"

"Mike broke his arm, in a match over at Gardena."

I grinned. "Mike plays for keeps, huh?"

She brushed the peat moss off her hands. "When he has to." She looked at me candidly. "I'll bet you do, too."

"When I have to," I admitted. "I get a feeling—Adonis isn't very well liked by his playmates."

She started to say something and stopped. She said, "Nobody's perfect."

"Be honest with me," I said lightly.

"Why?" She picked up the half-empty bag of peat moss. "Come into the house. I'm going to have a cup of coffee."

We went in through the side door. She put the peat moss in the service porch and led me into a white and blue kitchen with red flowered curtains on the windows. It was a highly feminine kitchen. And despite her size, she was a highly feminine woman.

She went over to get the coffee pot from the stove as I sat down in an upholstered breakfast nook. "Are you Greek?" she asked.

"Italian. Why?"

"You look Greek. Mike's a Greek."

I made no comment on that.

She took two cups from a cupboard. "He's a lot of man. So are you. Don't antagonize him, will you?"

"I'll try not to. Does he antagonize easily?"

"Lately he does. You know, Mike is probably the best

wrestler in the country? And I'll bet you've never heard of him."

"It's a big country," I said.

She laughed and poured my coffee. She said, "I'll bet you're fun at a party. Mike is. He can chin himself one hand. Can you chin yourself with one hand?"

"No." I sipped the coffee and smiled at her. "You know, it's entirely possible that if wrestling wasn't staged, Mike would be the heavyweight champion. And he might earn less as champion than he does now."

She nodded. "Mike said that's true. And he earns more than you'd guess by looking at this duplex. He's got four duplexes and two triplexes. That isn't enough for Mike."

"What does he want—office buildings?"

She shook her head gravely. "He wants to have pride in his trade."

I said nothing.

She said, "You're thinking it's a pretty crummy trade, even when it's honest."

I shrugged.

She said, "Well, so is yours. But I'll bet you take pride in it."

"At times," I said. "Like Mike does, at times. When we're both honestly playing policeman."

She stared at me. "Don't use that word to Mike."

"All right, I won't."

"Only one man would have told you that, only one man in the game, Adonis. You wouldn't want him laid up again, would you?"

I didn't answer.

She sipped her coffee and didn't look at me.

"Tell me," I said, "what did you think of Duncan Guest?"

She looked at me steadily. "He was slime. I can stand a homo. I can take the tough guys. I don't like men who take advantage of other men's weaknesses. Duncan Guest was a two hundred percent son-of-a-bitch."

There was the sound of the side door opening and in a few seconds a man came through the service porch doorway into the kitchen.

He was as tall as I am and about four inches broader. He had one cauliflower ear and a badly bent nose. His eyes were brown and friendly, his hair parted right down the middle.

He grinned at the big woman. "Back-dooring me, eh? You pick 'em big enough, don't you?"

"I have to," she said, "so they're not embarrassed. Mike, this is Joe Puma."

He frowned. "Puma? You ever wrestle?"

"Occasionally," I admitted. "But never with men." I stood up and offered my hand.

I could feel his strength even through the casual pressure of his handshake. I said, "I came to inquire into the death of Duncan Guest."

He stared at me. "Yuh? So why here?"

"Because," I ad libbed, "I thought his death might be connected with wrestling and I've been told you are the most honest man in the game."

"Who told you that?"

"My client," I lied.

"Adonis?"

I shook my head.

"Sit down," he said.

I sat down. He sat down. The woman poured him a cup of coffee. He took out a package of cigarettes and offered me one. I shook my head.

It was very quiet in the bright kitchen.

Finally, he asked, "Who's your client?"

"He's a wealthy man and he's connected with wrestling. I don't want to tell you any more than that."

"Okay." He took a deep breath. "I don't think Dunk's death had anything to do with wrestling. I think it's just the way the papers stated; I think he was killed by a woman."

"Why—?"

"How do I know why? He was a louse. He played both ends against the middle. He used people. Personally, I had nothing against him. I deal with bastards all the time; he was just another one. But some broads expect more from a man. Broads are harder to please than men, you know."

I sipped my coffee.

He asked, "Are you working for Curt Huntington?"

"I lied to you," I admitted. "I'm working for his sister."

"Oh." He stared at his housemate and back at me. "Know much about her?"

"Very little, except that she seems to be wealthy."

The woman said, "You're no scandal-monger, Mike."

He shook his head irritably. "I'm not saying anything he can't find out a dozen other places." He looked at me. "That Huntington girl was going with Duncan Guest. Some broad she must be, huh?"

"Love—" I said, and shrugged.

"Love," he said, and made a face. "You check her wardrobe, mister. I'll bet she's got a white dress and a cerulean mink stole. And enough money to buy all the alibis she wants."

"And enough of everything to get all the lovers she wants, too," I pointed out. "Why would she kill one?"

"Maybe Dunk found out something about her. That figures, right?"

"What could he find out?"

"Jesus, how would I know? A rich good-looking broad and she hangs around with scum. There must be something there an angle-shooter can milk a few bucks from, right? And if there was an angle, Duncan Guest would find it. That's how he lived."

The woman said, "You're getting all worked up, Mike. Relax."

He rubbed the back of his neck and stared at the table top. He looked up at me. "I suppose you see all kinds of trash, too."

"Some," I agreed. "Who's the big man in the wrestling game locally, Mike?"

"Right now," he answered, "Adonis is making the most money."

"That isn't what I meant," I said.

He nodded. "I know, I know. That was my answer. You won't get an answer to what you meant."

"Could I ask one more question?"

"Ask a million. I'm not going anyhere."

"I'll ask two. First, did Dunk ask you recently who the big man was?"

He paused. "He might have."

"And second, do you know Einar Hansen?"

He frowned. "The guy runs that hamburger joint?"

I nodded.

"I know him to say 'hello' to. Good friend of Dunk's."

"Okay, thanks." I stood up and looked at the woman. "I never did get your name."

She smiled. "Who needs it? Just think of me as Mike's woman." She winked. "This week."

He reached over to put a big hand on hers atop the table. "And every week. We'll get married, that's what."

"Why?" she asked. "This is more fun."

He patted her hand gently. "Don't talk like that."

FOUR

EINAR HANSEN sliced onions and said, "The funeral is tomorrow. You going?"

"No. I didn't know him. Do you remember what Deborah Huntington was wearing when Guest brought her in here?"

"Hell, yes. The police already asked me that. She was wearing a light blue sweater and skirt and a light blue gabardine topcoat. No hat. She's sure a beauty, huh?"

"She certainly is. Would you consider her a . . . well, I suppose I want to say *nice* girl?"

He looked up from the onions, his eyes watering. "Whatever that means. She was smart, pretty and not snobbish. How do I know if she was nice, whatever that means?"

"Would you consider Duncan Guest nice, whatever that means?"

He stepped back from the onions. He dried his eyes with a clean dish towel. "Duncan was my friend. We went all over that last time you were here. He played good chess and told good jokes and lent me money a couple of times and let me use his nookie haven. I don't know what kind of guy he was. To me, he was a good friend."

"Did you know that girl in the apartment next door, that Sheila Gallegan?"

He nodded. "I don't know her real well. I know her a little."

Behind us, the door opened, and two men came in. Both of them were shorter than I was and both of them were as broad. I wouldn't have been surprised to learn that both of them were tougher. They looked tougher.

They sat down a few stools from me. They could have been wrestlers, but I didn't think they were. They looked like a different brand of hoodlum.

Einar asked, "What'll it be, gents?"

"Just coffee," one of them said.

Einar looked at me and went over to pour two cups of coffee.

I said, "Well, I'll be seeing you again." I stood up.

One of the men turned to ask, "We're not rushing you, are we, dago?"

I faced him. "My name is Puma. No, you're not rushing me. Were you trying to?"

He turned to his twin and back to me. "No. Matter of fact, we just came in to cavesdrop. Your nose doesn't look as big as it is, does it?"

I stared at them and both of them now stared at me. From the corner of my eye, I could see Einar Hansen pick up the big knife he'd been slicing onions with. It was a razor-sharp knife.

He came over to stand in front of the men with the knife in his hand. He said calmly, "I'm skinny and non-combative, but I've been serving arrogant and muscle-bound creeps for seven years. And they've all learned not to mess with me. Now, I don't want any trouble in here."

They looked at Einar Hansen and at the knife. He looked at them with the noncommittal air of a man about to carve a turkey. He seemed at the moment less nervous than anyone in the place, including yours truly.

Then one of them laughed. He said, "We heard about you, Einar. We don't want any trouble with you, either. So we'll just go along with Puma."

Einar Hansen shook his head slowly. "No, you won't. He'll go now and you'll finish your coffee. You ordered it; you'll drink it."

Silence. Nobody moved. Even from outside, there was no sound.

One of the twins finally asked, "Aren't you crowding your luck a little bit, Einar? You made your play; don't milk it."

Einar said nothing.

The other man asked, "What's the wop to you?"

"A man on the right side of the law. And I'm a citizen." He lifted the knife. "I'm a respected business-man in this community."

"Shall I go?" I asked Einar. "Are you going to be all right?"

He nodded without taking his eyes from the men. "You go. I'm going to be all right."

I went out, leaving the tableau behind. I saw a blue Lincoln convertible parked on the lot near the stand and I took down the license number.

I drove mine off the lot quickly and parked it down a side street behind the Devon Tennis Club. I walked to the beach from there, and stayed out of sight where I could see the Lincoln.

In a few minutes, the two men came out and climbed into it. They drove away and I walked over to where I could see Hansen. He was again slicing onions.

I finally had a show of interest. Triggered by what? By my questioning of Mike Petalious? That seemed the most logical guess. I had talked with Adonis and Pe-talious and Hansen so far today. Hansen was out, which left—wait, I had forgotten yesterday. I had done some questioning then, too, though I hadn't known Duncan Guest was dead. Perhaps my yesterday's questioning had prompted this interest the hoods were now taking in me.

And perhaps Duncan Guest had followed this same inquisitive pattern to his death.

There was a tinge of smog in the air as I drove down Venice's Main Street. Usually, we don't get smog this far west of downtown, but the breeze was from the east today. It was hot in my Plymouth.

Duncan Guest, like everyone else, had been many things to many people. The Huntingtons and Einar Hansen liked him; Adonis liked him even more. Mike Petalious and his woman didn't share that sentiment. I wondered what Sheila Gallegan had thought of him.

She came to the doorway in a toweling robe over a swimsuit, her red hair pinned high on her head.

"Weren't you the man who was here yesterday?" she asked. "Aren't you the private detective who found him?"

"That's correct, Miss Gallegan. I'd like to ask you a few questions about him."

"I'm going to the beach," she said. "I haven't time for any questions. I've already told the police everything I know."

"Not everything," I told her. "You didn't tell them you were a friend of his. You lied about that."

She stared at me. She seemed to be holding her breath.

"I'm not planning to cause you any trouble," I said. "All I want is some information."

Her voice was edgy. "Who told you I was a friend of his?"

"Does it matter? I haven't told the police. There probably won't be any reason for me to ever tell the police."

"All right," she said finally. "Ask your questions." She came out a step and started to close the door behind her.

And from the apartment, a feminine voice said, "Bring him in, Sheila. He probably saw my car out there, anyway."

Sheila Gallegan shrugged and stepped back again, opening the door behind her. "Come in."

I came in to see Deborah Huntington sitting on an armless love seat, a cigarette in one hand and a highball in the other. She smiled at me. "You did see my car, didn't you?"

"I saw a Continental down there," I said, "but I didn't know you drove a Continental. Would it be impertinent of me to ask what in hell you're doing here?"

"I'm doing what you're doing,"- she answered. "I'm trying to learn about Duncan Guest. Though we have different reasons."

"Mine's money. What's yours?"

"Intellectual curiosity. The memory of the man refuses to die. He intrigues me more every minute. Have a drink?"

I looked inquiringly at Sheila Gallegan. She shrugged and said, "It's her liquor. She brought it."

I went to the kitchen sink to mix a drink. I brought it back and sat down in a wicker chair. I sipped it and asked Deborah Huntington, "You don't happen to have a white sheath dress, do you?"

"One or two," she admitted. "But among all my minks, I can't find a single cerulean stole."

"That isn't what I heard," I lied. "I heard only today that you had a heavenly cerulean mink stole." I had meanwhile learned that cerulean is a shade of blue.

She said evenly, "Either you're lying, or the person who told you that is lying. Which is it?"

"It must be the person who told me." I lifted my glass. "Do you want me to withdraw from the case, now that you're getting into the profession?"

She smiled. "Of course not. I'm sure you're much more competent than I could hope to be. What have you done today?"

Sheila Gallegan said, "You two don't need me, do you? I'd like to get to the beach."

I said, "I'd prefer to talk with you alone, Miss Gallegan, so I'll probably be back. But it would be presumptuous of us to stay here while you're away."

"Sheila doesn't mind," Deborah Huntington said easily. "Do you, Sheila?"

The girl shook her head. "Just close the door when you leave. It's a spring lock and I have a key. I'll be gone the rest of the day." She nodded and went out.

There was a silence for a moment after the door closed. Miss Huntington smoked and sipped her drink.

I said, "Are you a friend of Miss Gallegan's, or is today the first time you've met her?"

"Today is the first time we were really friendly. I've met her before."

I took a breath and asked, "When you were next door with Guest?"

She smiled. "Maybe. You're blushing a little."

"My peasant blood," I explained. "I always think of the female maidens of the upper classes as virginal."

She considered me quietly. Then she asked, "Learn anything?"

I told her about the people I had questioned. I told

her about the two men who had been in the hamburger stand.

She looked at me anxiously. "What does it mean? Who could they have been?"

"Muscles, working for the wrestling syndicate, I suppose. You see, I'm trying to get to Mr. Big in that dodge and I told Petalious that. He undoubtedly passed the word along. Well, if a Congressional committee were investigating, they wouldn't be that crude. But private operatives are considered expendable. By the hoodlums *and* the police."

She nodded in understanding, staring past me.

I said, "Now, do you want to tell me what you're doing here?"

"I told you, trying to get some information from Sheila." She paused. "And . . . well, maybe revisiting old scenes." Her face was suddenly bleak. "You know, I think I loved Duncan Guest." Her chin quivered.

"Easy," I said. "Don't build yourself into an alcoholic funk."

Her voice was rough. "All right, all right, all right. He was a tomcat, I know. But not since we met. For Christ's sake, could he help it if he was attractive to women?"

I shook my head and said calmly, "No. The part I'm beginning to despise him for was being attractive to *men.*"

She stared at me, her mouth open, her face slack. "No," she finally whispered.

"That's the way it looks," I said. "I've no proof, but it would be a safe bet. He is shaping up as an opportunist."

"No." She shook her head violently. "No!"

"Yes," I said.

She finished her drink and went to the kitchen to mix another. I called, "You're in a bad emotional state to start a binge."

"Shut up," she said. "I'll listen to my psychiatrist."

"You can't hide in a bottle," I said. "They're made of glass."

She came back to the living room with a full drink. It appeared to be about ninety percent whiskey. She said, "You're being very dull, Mr. Puma. You're not my adviser; you're just an employee."

"Yes'm," I said. "Are you going to the funeral?"

She shook her head. "I can't stand funerals. I didn't even go to my mother's."

Silence. She sipped her drink. I suddenly wanted another one. I lifted my empty glass and asked, "If you wouldn't mind?"

"Go ahead," she said. "It's cheap liquor."

I stood up. "It is, isn't it? And your brother mentioned something about your drinking it last night. Why?"

"It's a cheap habit," she said. "People who buy good liquor are making a cult out of a cheap escape. This much I like to believe about myself, I'm not phony."

I smiled. "Strange thing, I've known a lot of drunks. And eventually, if you're with them long enough, that line will come out—at least I'm not a phony. Why is that?"

Her face was blank. "I've no idea. I'll ask my psychiatrist. Go get your drink and shut up."

I went into the kitchen and mixed myself a drink. I brought it back to the living room and shut up. The silence hung in the room like fog. Dimly, from outside, we could hear the waves breaking on the beach.

Deborah Huntington started to cry.

I didn't move toward her. I sat where I was. She sat with head lowered, her drink in both hands in her lap, while the tears streamed down her face. She didn't sob or move.

After a few minutes I went to the bathroom and soaked a clean washcloth in cold water. I wrung it out and brought it to her. I took her drink from her.

She took the washcloth and wiped her face. She mumbled a thanks.

I said, "He wasn't worth that. I'm sure he wasn't."

She got up and went to the bathroom. I went to the window and looked down, expecting to see my two friends with the blue Lincoln convertible. But there was only my Plymouth and her black Continental below.

I'd see them again. Somewhere, they were undoubtedly waiting for me. *I always get the nasty ones*, I thought. *I always get the jobs where muscle is important. What a lousy racket.*

From behind me, she said, "What are you looking for?"

"Those broad and ugly men from the hamburger stand. I'm sure they haven't given up on me." I turned around.

Her face was puffed a little, but her lips were bright red again. She asked, "What makes you think Duncan's death was connected with wrestling? Are you overlooking that girl in the white dress entirely?"

"No, I'm not overlooking her. But I'm sure Duncan Guest made enough enemies in the wrestling game to warrant some investigation there. And I'm sure the wrestlers he knew might give me a lead to his love life. Which would bring me back to the girl in the white dress. She could be somebody's wife, you know."

"Some rich man's wife, and Duncan was blackmailing her?"

I shrugged. "What made you think of blackmail? Did he try it with you?"

"Of course not. How could he?" Her chin lifted. "My reputation isn't good enough to be valuable, Mr. Puma."

"Do you cherish that bad reputation?"

She studied me calmly. "Why do we have to wrangle all the time? God, isn't there enough friction in the world?"

"You're right," I said. "I'm sorry."

"You're a lot like Curt," she said, "do you know that? You're remote. You're—insulated."

I shook my head. "That's the last thing I am. I'm Italian. I bleed easily."

"All right, then," she said, "call it self-sufficient."

"I've had to be," I said. "I made my own way since I was twelve. I put myself through college. I ask no favors. And I don't like to be asked favors. Except by friends."

"Call me a friend, Puma, and take me to dinner, then." She paused. "I'll pay."

"It's too early for dinner. Let's sit and talk for a while. Should we go to the beach?"

"All right. But I'm paying for the dinner, remember."

"No," I said.

"I insist," she said.

"I'm not a flunky," I said. "I'll pay for the dinner. Now, shut up."

She looked up and smiled. "You don't even know how to say 'shut up.' Don't you ever say it?"

"Not as often as you do," I told her. "Let's go look at the water. It's a great sedative."

There was not only the water. There was the sun and a nice breeze from the ocean, and dozens of bathers. Toward the north, Muscle Beach was visible, and even at this distance I could see the bulbous calves and biceps of the cavorting freaks.

We brought a blanket from her car and sat on the sand and talked of everything but death. We talked about Malibu and Balboa, about Arrowhead and Venice, about Hemingway, Cozzens, Frost, Algren, Kazan, Stevens and Brando. She tried to take me up to Camus, Gide, and Kafka but that was a foreign country to me, so we came back to Steinbeck and Saroyan.

Nice clean talk and I enjoyed every second of it but was aware of her through all those enjoyable seconds. It is one of my curses—I always exist at two levels around attractive women.

Sex appeal oozed out of her, and I wondered if that was what had sent her to a psychiatrist. She was attractive and probably vulnerable. In this town, or any town, it's a regrettable combination.

At six o'clock she said, "Aren't you hungry yet? I'm starved."

I nodded and helped her up.

She said, "Look, the reason I wanted to pay, I want to eat some nice place, some expensive place. And—"

"I'm earning a hundred dollars a day," I told her. "I can handle it."

"*Two* hundred today? All right?"

"God damn it," I said, "shut up!"

She smiled. "You're learning how to say it. You're getting better. Race you to the car."

She had her shoes in her hand and she made pretty good time through that heavy sand. I let her win. I figured it was good for her to win once in a while.

We ate in Cini's in Beverly Hills. She wanted to leave her car where it was, but I explained to her how fast a parked Continental would be stripped in Venice, once the sun went down. So we took both cars to Cini's.

They have the best Italian food in America at Cini's, and people who should know have told me it's superior to the Italian food in Italy, too.

Deborah wanted to know how a crummy private eye could afford to know about a place like this, and I explained that even the crummiest of us occasionally get millionaire clients.

We ate and drank Vino Cini and talked about a number of trivial things. And toward the end of the meal, she asked again, "Why aren't you concentrating on the girl in the white sheath dress? Don't you believe Sheila Gallegan?"

"Not completely."

"She seems to be a very nice girl."

"Mmmm-hmmm. But even if she did see the girl in the white sheath dress, does it follow that the girl was the murderer? Couldn't it be possible that the killer was just waiting for the girl to leave? Where can I start looking for an unidentified girl? First I want the pattern of Guest's life. Murder needs a motive, Deborah."

"How about the thump and the scream?"

I told her, "If all the thumps and screams one hears at night in Venice would indicate murder, there'd be no residents left."

She shook her head. "You're not making sense. You're not making sense at all."

"Murder never does," I told her. "It's not a rational act."

"Let's talk about something else," she said.

It was a long meal and a full one and we sat for some time after that. At nine o'clock, I suggested leaving.

Her gaze held mine. "I don't want to go home. Couldn't I come to your place for a while?"

That was plain enough. And I thought of Petalious and his woman and remembered their scorn for this girl and some latent integrity stirred in me, but I was still more man than saint.

I said, "I guess. It's not much of a place." My voice shook.

"You think I'm cheap, don't you?"

"I think you're honest. Do you think you're cheap?" She nodded.

"Well, then don't come to my place."

"I want to," she said. "I have to."

She followed me home in the big black Continental. She went up the stairs with me to my utilitarian apart-

ment and looked around and said, "For a man, you keep
it very clean."

"I grew up doing my own housekeeping."

She went to the window and looked out. Then she
came over to stand in front me, looking up. I pulled
her close and kissed her and she whimpered softly, her
body pressed hungrily to mine.

"There are worse compulsions," I said.

"Aren't there, though? Are you gentle, Joe Puma?"

"Usually. I don't like to be considered a sedative,
though."

"You're not, you're not, you're not—" She squirmed
free to look at me. "I want to take a shower, first."

I nodded. "Be my guest."

I went to the window as she went to the bathroom.
I thought again of Mike Petalious, that moral man who
was almost married. That moral man who was hired
to keep wrestling crooked. What right did that bastard
have to a moral judgment?

And why should his opinions bother me?

She came out finally, rounded and tanned and fragrant,
and I didn't think about Mike Petalious any more.

FIVE

SHE LEFT before midnight, and I sat up for a while,
drinking a can of beer and thinking back on the day.
The Gallegan girl was a possible key; I would have to
get back to her.

The muscular twins hadn't followed up their original
threat and I wondered why. My address was in the
phone book. Had they been called off, or did they
presume they had scared me off the hunt? I couldn't
be sure my visit to Petalious had triggered them. My
name had been in the paper yesterday as the man who
had found Duncan Guest's body. And they knew Adonis
had hired me.

Mike had broken Adonis' arm, a little item Adonis had
never mentioned to me. Had Adonis tried to win one

he wasn't scheduled to win? That seemed like the reason for the broken arm, but it had never been stated; I had inferred it from the knowledge that Petalious was the policeman.

I slept right through until nine o'clock and was wakened by the phone. It was Sergeant Macrae.

"We've had a small beef on you, Puma," he told me.

"From whom, Sergeant?"

"From a man named Mike Petalious. Know him?"

"I talked with him yesterday. What's his beef? He was friendly enough then."

"He couldn't understand why he had to be bothered by a private investigator. He said if the Department had reason to question him, they should send an authorized man to do it."

"I didn't twist his arm. Sergeant. I wouldn't try to. He's tougher than I am."

"He must be some man. Why did you question him, Puma?"

"Because I heard he was the man who took care of any wrestler who got ambitious. I was trying to find out who gave him his orders."

"I don't follow you."

I said, "In the trade, they call him the policeman. Any wrestler who decides he'd rather try to win than follow the predetermined routine of a bout is matched with Petalious. And Petalious puts him back on the crooked and narrow."

"You're telling me wrestling is actually fixed?"

"Do I have to? My God, you've got a television set, haven't you?"

"Sure. But I don't watch wrestling. My wife does, though, and I'd hate to tell her it's fixed. She'd scalp me."

I said nothing as there was nothing to say.

He said, "Wouldn't that be information for the Boxing and Wrestling Commission?"

"It certainly wouldn't be news to them. And I'm not working for them. I'm trying to help you, Sergeant."

"I'll bet. Who gave you the lead to Petalious?"

"Adonis Devine."

"Did you make a report of all this?"

"Not yet. I will, as soon as I get to the office."

There was a silence. Then Macrae said musingly, "I wonder why Petalious phoned us?"

"I imagine he was told to. By someone a little brighter than he is. And I imagine this brighter person knew you Department men loathe and despise private operatives. And I can assume from that this bright man would expect you to tell me to keep my big nose out of the case. Is that what you phoned to tell me?"

"But why in hell should he fear you if he doesn't fear us?"

"Sergeant," I said humbly, "modesty forbids my answering that question."

Another silence. Then, "Smart, aren't you?"

"No, sir."

"Okay, Puma, stay with it. And make carbons of each daily report. And mail them to me every day."

"Yes, Sergeant. Thank you."

"And don't be so God-damned humble. On you, it looks bad."

"Check," I said. "Right!"

I hung up and went to the bathroom to shave. So that was why the belligerent pair hadn't followed up their initial threat of yesterday. An easier way to get rid of Puma had been dreamed up by someone.

I poached three eggs and placed them neatly on raisin bread toast. Silly combination, but I have always liked it. I made tea instead of coffee, this morning. It is little changes like these that add color to the drab life of the poor and lonely.

The *Times* informed me that the "mysterious mink-garbed murderess" was still a mystery to the police but new leads from Department informants had made the investigating officers optimistic of imminent revelations. That meant there was nothing new on the case.

In a day or so, another murder would come along; they always did. And this one would be forgotten. Duncan Guest had not been a very important man.

I went to the office and typed up the report for yesterday, making a copy for Sergeant Macrae. The *Herald-Express* identified the girl as the "woman in white" and I liked that better than "mink-garbed murderess." The *Times* is really too dignified to be success-

fully trashy. Though they certainly achieve it in their
sport pages.

I went from the office to the Wilshire Arena. Offices
fronting on the Boulevard were a part of the structure
and Gregory Harvest, Attorney-at-Law, had one of the
offices. He must have moved in there recently. I didn't
stop in to see him.

I went in past a pair of sweating, grunting monsters
in the gym to the balcony office of Curtis Huntington,
President of Huntington Properties, Inc.

A capable-looking woman of about fifty in the outer
office told me Mr. Huntington was in and she would
check to see if he was busy.

He wasn't busy, and she ushered me into a dim and
paneled office a minute later. The dapper, elegant brother
of my client was in gray flannel today, a fabric soft as
mist and delicate as a maiden's dream.

"Mr. Puma," he said. "What have you learned?"

"Very little. I thought you might be able to help."

"Sit down," he said. "Drink?"

"Not in the morning, thanks. I talked with Mike
Petalious yesterday."

"So?"

"I heard he was what is known in the trade as the
'policeman.' Is that correct?"

Curt Huntington put the tips of his fingers together.
"That's correct. Mike's the best wrestler in the business.
Though I guess that doesn't mean much, today."

"He was friendly enough yesterday, but after I left,
he complained to the police about my visit."

Huntington smiled. "Somebody up there didn't like it."

"That's what I figured. Who's up there?"

"I don't really know," Huntington said. "The question
has intrigued me from time to time, but never enough
to prompt an investigation by me. I could find out,
though, I'm sure."

"Would you? For me?"

Huntington nodded.

I said, "Somebody else told me yesterday that Duncan
Guest was obsessed with the absurd idea that honest
wrestling might pay. Just as a change."

"You were told the truth. I even encouraged Duncan.

Not that wrestling of any kind interests me, but I had a lot of faith in his judgment. You see, boxing once a week is about the best I can hope for in the Arena, and wrestling receipts were falling off. Duncan was a gifted promotional man."

"You don't think Guest could have been killed because he pursued this idea?"

Huntington shook his head. "Of course not. However, it's entirely possible he might have learned something else in pursuing the idea, something not connected with the obvious dishonesty of wrestling."

I stared at the window.

Huntington asked, "Did you question Adonis yesterday?"

I nodded.

"A strange man, isn't he?"

I looked up. "Did you mean queer, or strange?"

"I meant strange. He's no longer queer, I understand."

"He cried," I said, "when I broke the news to him of Duncan's death."

"I saw him cry in a ring, once," Huntington said thoughtfully.

"The night Petalious broke his arm?"

"Yes. But *before* Petalious broke his arm. He was crying because of frustration. Mike made him look pitiful."

"Adonis wrestled in college," I explained. "Perhaps he thought he really had it."

"Quite a few have thought so, before they were matched with Mike. Did you meet Mike's girl friend?"

"Big woman?"

He nodded. "And from a big family. She was a Quintana and I'm sure that name's as big as any in town. Old California money and Mike wouldn't take a nickel of it."

It was a name even bigger than Huntington. I said, "Neither of them think much of Duncan Guest."

Curtis Huntington smiled. "Mike takes his trade too seriously. And Mike's attitudes are always his wife's. He's her personal god."

I stood up. "Well, you try to find out the name I want. I'll call you. And thanks for your time."

"Don't mention it," he told me genially. "Time is one thing I have plenty of."

Time and money, I thought. What a life. It was enough to make a Democrat out of a man. I went out through the gym and there were a few more hams grappling now, and I stood for a minute, watching them. They put on a better show here than they ever did for the public. Perhaps in all of them lurked the unadmitted belief that they could actually wrestle. Perhaps the workouts in the gym were the only solace in their days. Except for the money.

Outside, I stood for a moment on the curb as a Jaguar slid into a parking spot.

The man looked up and I saw it was Gregory Harvest. "Just a minute, Joe," he called. "I want to talk with you."

He had sent me some business, but we had never been real friends. I waited while he parked, wondering what angle he was cooking up now.

He'd been a hot-shot halfback at SC and a first-rate college poker player. On graduation from law school, he had gone to work first for one of the local, conservative investment firms. Once his beguiling personality had endeared him to the money families, he had started his own law firm. He had a very alert eye for the main chance and it was probably envy that made me dislike him faintly.

He came along the sidewalk frowning and I waited with a smile. "I hope you have a minute," he said. "I'd like to talk with you in my office."

"I'm pretty busy," I said grudgingly, "but I guess I can spare a minute."

He studied me for a second, a muscle flexing in his jaw, like the heavy in a B picture. He continued toward his office without a word and I went along.

We went through a silver and gray reception room to a gray and maroon private office. There, he went to the water cooler and drank three cups full of water.

Then he sat down behind his desk and nodded toward a chair at the side of the desk. I sat in that.

He leaned back, looking thoughtful and not looking at me. He was as much of a ham as any wrestler in that gym.

"I can't be that important," I said.

He looked at me and smiled absently. "I'm searching for—diplomatic phrasing of some words that need to be said."

"Don't try too hard," I said. "I'm not sensitive."

He had a fairly round face and curly chestnut hair. The combination should have made him look cherubic but it never had. He somehow looked like what he was —a shrewd, cool operator.

"Now," he said quietly, "I sense that you don't always approve of me, Joe, but I have a lot of regard for your talents and I intend to use them whenever it makes good business sense."

"Thank you," I said. "That's very comforting. It isn't disapproval you sense in me, it's envy."

He smiled cooly. "Well, thank *you*. In this current unpleasantness, however, perhaps you were a bad choice for the job."

"I wasn't your choice," I reminded him. "Remember, when you phoned me, you told me Deborah Huntington had seen my name in the paper and she wanted me called in."

"I know, I know," he said impatiently. "I didn't say this was *my* bad choice. I said perhaps you were *a* bad choice."

"By God, you did," I said admiringly. "I never would have made a lawyer, would I, Greg?"

The muscle in his jaw flexed again. He didn't like humor from inferiors, particularly bad humor. He said, "Discretion and dignity, those should be the dominant motifs in this investigation."

"She picked a bad man for those," I admitted. "Where did I fail, Greg?"

He stared at me quietly. I had a feeling we were about to get to the meat of this conversation. But he said nothing.

So I asked, "Were you a particular friend of Duncan Guest's?"

"A casual friend. I'm a very good friend of Deborah Huntington's, Joe. I—I'm very, very fond of her."

The word "love" he couldn't use. Psychic block? Her money he was very, very fond of.

"She's a wonderful girl," I said.

"She's a vulnerable girl," he answered.

And aren't those the kind you like best? I thought.
Rich, pretty and vulnerable girls? I said nothing.

"She was under psychiatric treatment for almost a
year," he went on. "That's a family secret and I'm
breaking a confidence. I wanted to impress on you
the importance of your behaving with discretion and
dignity."

"I'm not sure," I said slowly, "whether you're warning
me or reprimanding me."

"Both, Joe. And my advice is respected by the Huntingtons. A word from me and you'd be off this case
immediately."

I shrugged. "So give 'em the word. What do you want
from me?"

He took a breath. He leaned forward with his forearms
on the desk. "I had a date with Deborah last night."

"Have fun? Where'd you go?"

His round face was like a marble. "She didn't make
it. She didn't phone and break it. She simply didn't
make it."

"That's awful God-damned tough," I said, "but I'm
not Dorothy Dix. What's it to me whether she made it
or not?"

"Don't be arrogant," he said. "Don't think your—Latin
charm has you in so solid you can't be replaced."

I stood up. "You're talking like a child. I've just come
from Curtis Huntington's office, so I know he's there.
Let's go in and you can tell him you want me off the
case. And you can tell him why. Or I will. Let's go."

He sat there glaring at me, making no move.

I smiled. "If I showed two small pairs right now, or
even a pair of kings, you'd run and hide, wouldn't you?"

"You arrogant—" He expelled his breath.

"Dago?" I supplied. "Look, even if you did get me
thrown off the case, there's still that three grand Adonis
has posted. And I'm not busy on anything else right
now. You'd still be investigated, along with the rest."

"Get out of here," he said hoarsely. "You'll hear from
the Huntingtons, I guarantee you."

"Calm down, for Christ's sake," I said. "You're acting
way out of character, Greg. You're making an ass of
yourself."

"Get out," he said almost shrilly. "Get out right now!"

The door behind me opened, and his secretary stuck her head in. "Is everything all right, Mr. Harvest?"

"Close that damned door!" he shouted.

The door closed quickly and I stood there, watching him breathe, meeting his glare with wonder.

"A time may come," he said evenly, "when I decide to find out exactly how tough you are. I met a few tough ones at SC, you might remember."

I shook my head. "Relax, halfback. You need the men with whistles, the men with the penalty flags." *And you need your mother*, I thought. A mama's boy, he had been.

"Will you go now?" he asked in a subdued voice.

"Of course," I said. "And I apologize if it was my insolence that gave you your seizure." I nodded and went out.

The secretary glared at me as I went through the outer office. I said, "Mr. Harvest asked me to tell you to get Curtis Huntington on the phone. He has some important information for him."

She stared at me rigidly. "I'll check with Mr. Harvest first, sir, if you don't mind."

"You were listening," I accused her gently. "You were eavesdropping again. I'm a detective and I can tell."

She colored slightly and went back to her typing, ignoring me.

I went out into an overcast day. It was almost noon but the sun hadn't broken through yet. I thought about the smooth Gregory Harvest. He had acted like a high school boy in love, a jealous high school boy. Could a man get that furious over something as dull as money?

He couldn't believe his beloved was a virgin; it had to be the money that infuriated him. Or perhaps I had not been properly servile and his momentary loss of dominance had cracked him. It had been a side of him I had never expected to see, I wouldn't have believed existed.

Strong and angry men don't frighten me nearly as much as weak and angry men. The weak ones have too much to prove to themselves and it extends them beyond sanity. The thought of Greg Harvest made me uneasy.

I ate lunch in Santa Monica and drove over to Venice

from there. I didn't stop to chat with Einar Hansen to-day. I could see the sign on the door. The place was closed; Einar had undoubtedly gone to Duncan Guest's funeral. That had been scheduled for this morning.

I continued toward the heart of Venice, toward the apartments over the four-car garage.

The red-head was parking an ancient and battered Chev as I pulled into the vacant lot next to the garage. She was in deep blue with a hat and gloves, demure and formal. She stood waiting for me as I came across the lot.

She said nothing, studying me.

"Shopping?" I asked.

"I was at the funeral. Your friend was there. Miss Huntington. Why don't you talk to her about Duncan Guest?"

"Rich people hold things out on me. They don't always tell the truth. Of course, for all I know, you're rich, too."

"Rich? And living here?"

"You don't work," I explained. "I was here yesterday and the day before and you were home."

"I work nights," she told me.

"Oh?" I smiled. "You *were* a friend of Duncan's, weren't you? Or you wouldn't have gone to his funeral."

"I was a friend of Duncan's," she admitted quietly, "for about a week and a half. I was more than a friend for that week and a half."

"He must have been a charming man," I said. "I'm sorry I never met him while he was alive."

She said wearily, "You may as well come up. There's still some of Deborah Huntington's whiskey in the cup-board."

I said jokingly, "You sound jealous."

"Don't give it a thought," she said. "You're not my type at all. You big, sweaty slobs are repugnant to me."

I laughed as we walked up the steps. I said, "The start of a beautiful friendship."

Before we got to her door, she was smiling.

I sat in the wicker chair while she went to the kitch-enette. She called, "Is 7-Up all right with it?"

"Just tap water," I said.

She mixed hers with 7-Up and mine with tap water.

She had taken off her hat and gloves and the golden red of her hair was haloed by the afternoon sun.

I thanked her and leaned back in the chair. I said, "Guest must have had a lot of girls over in that operating room of his."

She sat on the armless love seat. "He had a lot of girls everywhere, I imagine."

"Who followed you?" I asked. "Who took your place?"

She was quiet a moment. And then she said softly, "Deborah Huntington."

"And yesterday, you and Deborah were sorting out old memories, or something like that?"

She didn't answer. She sat there looking at me dully.

I asked, "Did Duncan ever have any of his boy friends over there?"

She frowned. "I'm not sure I understand you."

"I'm sure you do."

She sipped her drink and looked past me. "That was a side of Duncan's life I'd heard about but was not familiar with. There were men there from time to time."

"Had you heard about that side of his life *before* you started to go with him?"

Her chin lifted and I saw her stiffen but she didn't answer.

"I'm not judging you," I explained.

"You'd better not."

"And I'm not investigating you," I went on. "Nor trying to invade your privacy. I'm simply searching for a murderer."

She nodded.

"Do you know Einar Hansen?"

"Yes. As a matter of fact, I've gone out with him once or twice. Don't tell me he's double-gaited too?"

"I'm sure he isn't. I don't know him very well, but I like what I've seen of him. And yet, he claims to have been a very good friend of Duncan Guest's. I should think Einar would have more discernment."

"How about Miss Huntington? How about me? A lot of fairly decent people liked Duncan Guest. I've heard that his best friend, this wrestler who offered the reward, is a very fine man."

"And where did you hear that?"

"'Around. I don't remember. It's—common knowledge."

"Maybe. Uncommon knowledge, maybe. I'm a—little biased about wrestlers. I could be wrong about Devine."

"You could be wrong about Deborah Huntington, too, couldn't you?"

"Certainly. I've no illusions about her, if that's what you mean. I guess I'm just naturally compassionate."

She said stiffly, "I have a friend on the Santa Monica Police Force who insists that private investigators are the nastiest, meanest, most dishonest people alive."

I laughed. "He must be the man who gave you the character reference on Devine. Miss Gallegan, some of us are almost human. And most of us are closer to it than anyone in a certain police department I won't mention. You could be as wrong about me as I'm sure you were about Duncan Guest. I can give you any number of better references than your friend on the Santa Monica Police Force."

She sipped her drink and said nothing.

I asked, "Don't you want Duncan's murderer to be found?"

Her eyes flared. "Of course! What a nasty question!"

"You're not very co-operative."

"I was co-operative with the police." She paused. "I'm —not sure you're on the same side, Mr. Puma."

"Phone Captain Bixby down at Headquarters," I told her. "Phone Sergeant Macrae right here in Venice. I'm working completely with the Los Angeles Police Department on this murder."

"Then you must have access to the information I gave them. And why are you questioning me?"

"Because," I explained, "I'm still a *private* investigator. And certain important facts that might point to a killer remain a secret with me, so long as they don't interfere with justice. The Department can't be that discreet. They need the support of the newspapers and the newspapers relish those indiscreet, circulation-building bits of smear the private man withholds from them."

"Or sells to a scandal magazine," Sheila Gallegan added.

"Ouch!" I said. "That was a fair blow, but still painful. Would you like another drink?"

"Why? What good would that do you? I'm not Deborah Huntington."

I stood up. "You keep telling yourself. I'll bet you'd like to be."

She glared at me and her voice was shaky. "Don't bother to mix yourself another drink."

"I didn't intend to." I looked at her coolly. "I'm going. I apologize for my insolence. But you've been—frustrating. Take care of yourself." I went to the door.

I opened it and looked down across the runway and a pair of faces looked right back at me. Faces I had seen only once before. The malevolent twins were standing in the empty lot below, watching this door.

I closed it.

SIX

"CALL THE POLICE," I told Sheila Gallegan, and she looked up, startled.

"No, wait," I added. "Maybe they only want to talk. Maybe I'd learn more if you didn't call the police."

"Who?" she asked. She stood up. "What's the matter?"

"A couple of—hoodlums who tried to start a fight with me in Hansen's place yesterday are standing down in that lot. I'm sure they're waiting for me."

She stared at me and swallowed.

I said quietly, "You can watch them through that window. If they start to get rough, or I start to walk off with them, call the police. I won't walk off with them under my own volition."

She chewed her lower lip. "Do you think thats wise? Wouldn't it be better to call the police right now?"

"No, Sheila. That's what I was trying to explain to you before. They might say things to me they wouldn't say to the police. That's my edge, you see."

She took a deep breath. "Are you armed?"

"No. You don't happen to have a gun around, do you?"

"I have a knife, a hunting knife, sharp as a razor."

"I'm not good with a knife," I told her. "You watch from the window, now."

She nodded. She put a hand on my arm. "Be careful, won't you?"

I grinned at her. "I knew, under that protective mask, you really cared, Irish. Now, don't blank out on me if things get rough down there. You're my liaison man; you're my best hope."

"You're a damned idiot," she said, "but be careful."

I opened the door and went out. I closed the door behind me and looked down at my friends and waved.

They looked up and smiled. One string could have worked both smiles.

It was like one of those western movies where the hero goes out into the lonely street to meet the man at the far end. Only it was two men I was meeting, not one man. And maybe they only wanted to talk.

I only wanted to talk.

It was early afternoon and all of the lot was visible from the street and from the dwelling on every side. It didn't seem reasonable that they would try any rough stuff, but hoodlums aren't inclined toward reason. That's what makes them hoodlums.

I went down the steps with the faint taste of brass in my mouth and a slight tremor in my knees. I came around the bottom of the steps and walked toward my car and they were waiting next to it.

They had no unusual distinguishing features. The brown eyes of one were a little lighter than the brown eyes of the other.

When I was about four feet from the car, Light-brown said, "You're a busy man, aren't you?"

I nodded. "I expected to see you boys earlier than this. You were called off for a while, weren't you?"

Light-brown looked at Dark-brown. "Hep, ain't he?"

They were both standing in front of the front door of my car, now, on the driver's side.

I said, "Whatever your business is, get it over with."

They moved a few feet apart. Light-brown said, "We wouldn't hold you up. Get into your car. We'll go along."

"No," I said. "And if you're armed, you're making a stupid play. You'll never get away with it."

"Why not?" Dark-brown asked.

"Because," I said, "I've already given your license number to Sergeant Macrae at the Venice Station. Call him, if you don't believe that."

Light-brown looked up at the runway. "You couldn't read our license number from up there."

"I know. I gave it to him yesterday. I took it when you were parked next to Hansen's hamburger stand."

They both looked doubtful.

Light-brown nodded and the other man stepped further away. Light-brown said, "Take off, then, Puma. We'll get to you again."

That would be a sucker play, walking between them now. I stood where I was and said, "I'll go when you go."

Light-brown smiled. "I told you he was a wise guy. Careful man, ain't you?"

"I have to be," I said. "Petalious send you boys?"

They both stared at me. Then Dark-brown looked up at the runway and said to his pal, "'Maybe we can slap some answers out of the red-head up there. Maybe the dago told her something."

"Boys," I said evenly, "she's a lamb. She's a noncombatant. And if anything should happen to her, I would consider it my personal duty to find you two."

Dark-brown smiled again. "Oh, tough, huh? Why is your voice shaking if you're so tough?"

"From anger," I said. "I know I'm tougher than any man who needs a partner for a play."

"Leave me have him," Dark-brown said angrily. "Leave me have him all alone." He moved closer to me, on my right.

I waited, watching them both. I misjudged the man on my left. He came in fast and he came in hooking. I backhanded him with my left and and swung a right at the other one coming in from that side.

It was a fine start. Light-brown went stumbling to one side and Dark-brown caught my fist right smack in the middle of his teeth. I got him in the neck with a left hand before Light-brown regained his footing.

And then I made a tactical error. I figured Light-brown deserved the immediate attention as Dark-brown had just caught two good, stiff punches. Dark-brown's mouth was bleeding and he seemed to be wavering.

I turned to Light-brown and he circled further to my left, bringing my attention around that way. And exposing the right side of my head to Dark-brown.

I saw him move in, but his partner moved in at the same time and I concentrated on him—as the man to my right sapped me behind the ear.

I went down half-conscious and caught a foot in the throat. I heard the wail of a siren right after they started to kick me.

There was this angel coming out of the water, wet and with her wings bedraggled, and she came closer and tried to shake her wings dry and the water poured all over me and ran down my neck under my open collar.

And I opened my eyes to look into the eyes of Sheila Gallegan. I was lying on one of those beds that pull out of the wall, and she was bathing my face with a wet towel. She was pale and the hand holding the towel trembled.

I smiled at her. I looked past her into the thoughtful stare of Sergeant Macrae.

"We brought you up here," he said. "Your injuries didn't look serious, so we carried you up here. The boys got away." He paused. "Do you know who they were?"

I tried to talk and only a whisper came out. My vocal cords must have been bruised by that kick. I managed, "I put their license number into a report I mailed you this morning. Maybe you didn't get it yet."

"I didn't. What were you doing at Miss Gallegan's, here?"

I nodded toward her and made a face.

She said, "He was questioning me about the murder."

Macrae was silent for seconds. Then he asked me, "Do you need a doctor?"

I shrugged and put a finger to the lump over my ear. "Concussion?"

"It's possible. I'll call a doctor."

"Wait," I said. "Maybe I won't need one. Let me rest for a few minutes."

He nodded and sat down on a pull-up chair near the bed. "Who do you think sent those slobs after you?"

"I don't know. One man you could question is Mike Petalious. Not that he'd tell you anything."

"The man they call the 'policeman'?"

I nodded.

He chewed his lip. "Miss Gallegan told me you saw those men out there before you went down the steps. Why didn't you call the police first?"

I whispered, "I explained that to Miss Gallegan and I'm sure you had her explain it to you."

"Yes," he admitted. "I just wanted you to confirm it. What makes you think I gave you permission to work *outside* the law?"

"Be reasonable, Sergeant. All your informants work outside the law. If you didn't have them, there'd be no law, only chaos."

He stared at me for seconds and then stood up and went to the phone. Sheila Gallegan went to get me a glass of water.

On the phone, Macrae said, "Pick up Mike Petalious. Bring him in and hold him. That's right, over in Brentwood; you know where he lives."

The water felt good, going down my sore throat. I put my hands beneath me and rose to a sitting position. The pain in my stomach muscles brought sweat to my forehead.

Macrae asked anxiously, "How about internal injuries? You're bone-white, man."

"They must have kicked me in the belly," I said. My voice was better.

Macrae said, "You wouldn't happen to remember that license number, would you?"

I reached into my jacket pocket and took out my notebook and the number was still there. I handed it to him. He went to the phone again.

Sheila Gallegan said, "You damned idiot! Why did you do what you did?"

"Every once in a while," I told her gently, "I feel the need for a test. You see, I'm one of those dopes more physical than mental and there's no other way I can be sure I'm alive."

She shook her head vexedly. "Sarcastic, too. Idiotic, sarcastic, arrogant and—" She expelled her breath angrily.

"And attractive to women," I added coyly. "Don't bleed for me, honey."

She glared at me.

Macrae came from the phone to ask, "What'd they say to you? Did they say anything about Miss Gallegan here?"

I hesitated.

His stare was hard. "The truth, now."

I answered, "All they said was that maybe they'd be luckier if they came up here and slapped some answers out of her."

"And that's why you started to swing?"

I shrugged. "Partly."

Sheila Gallegan colored. She rose and went into the kitchen.

Macrae winked at me. "Score me for an assist, Romeo." He shook his head. "You're a hard man to hate."

"Why try, Sergeant?" I asked him. "I've got my freedom but you've got your pension. We're both doing the Lord's work."

"That's sacrilege," he said. "Watch your tongue."

I took a deep breath. I could see Sheila Gallegan in the kitchen. She was drinking a glass of water. I ached all over. I itched to meet the brown-eyed bastards again. *But one at a time*, I warned myself; *you're not Superman, Puma*. Discretion and favorable odds are the same ingredients in valor.

"Who are you hating now?" Macrae asked. "I wish I had a mirror for you."

"Who would you hate, Sergeant, if you were sitting here now?"

"You take it easy," he warned me. "When we drag 'em in, maybe we can trip 'em a few times, but I don't want your wop . . . Italian temper getting the best of you."

"You can say 'wop,'" I told him. "You're my friend."

"You want to be my friend, you got to earn it, Puma. I'm the law and don't you forget it. You're not the law."

"You're badly educated, Sergeant. I'm the law. Any righteous citizen is the law."

His voice was rough. "Righteous! You? Start over."

"I'm righteous in my way. You don't have to worry about me, Sergeant."

"Your voice is back," he said sourly. "Why didn't I leave while you were still whispering?"

I didn't answer him. Sheila Gallegan came from the kitchen with two aspirin tablets and a glass of water. I took them like a lamb.

She asked softly, "Do you think those men will come back?"

Macrae said, "We'll keep a close watch on your place, Miss Gallegan."

Sure they would. With what? They didn't have enough men now to half cover the town. I said, "I guess I won't need a doctor. My head doesn't ache much any more."

"Okay," he said. "I've got plenty to do. You'll be all right, Miss Gallegan. Don't you worry about it."

He went out. I heard him talk to some reporters at the door. In less than a minute, there was complete silence.

Sheila Gallegan studied me vexedly. "Why did you have to be insolent with *him*, too? He was very nice."

"Because," I explained, "he was about to tell me to get the hell out of the case. And I learned early in life that the best defense is a fast and angry offense. Offensive, you see, is a word that is supposed to have two meanings, but both meanings are really the same."

"You have a lot of answers, don't you?" she said quietly. "You've always got an answer."

"Because I'm rational." I swung my legs around and sat on the edge of the bed. "Do you think I like arguments? Do you think I enjoy violence?"

"Yes," she said clearly.

"Jesus," I said wearily, "nobody understands me. *Nobody!*"

"Except for Miss Huntington?" she suggested.

I glared at her. "Get off that kick, will you? Get off that envious, adolescent, idiotic, obsessive resentment against Deborah Huntington. It's like a cancer in you."

She stared at me, her chin trembling, her blue eyes misting.

"Cry," I said. "You've held it too long."

She began to cry. I went to the window and looked out at the traffic on the street. I went to the other window and looked out at the empty lot next door. Not a cop in sight.

She was sitting in the pull-up chair now, with her head forward on the bed and crying whole-heartedly.

I went into the kitchen and mixed myself a drink. I went into the bathroom and took a couple tissues from her Kleenex box.

The crying had diminished some when I came back into the living room. I tapped her shoulder and she looked up. I handed her the tissues.

She stared for a few seconds and then blew her nose. She said, "You could have mixed me a drink, too, you big dago."

I smiled. "That's better. Now you're talking like the Irish should. Take this one."

She took my drink and I went back to get another one. When I returned to the living room, she was sitting erectly in the pull-up chair.

"One question," she said. "What has that Huntington girl got that I haven't got?"

"For men?"

She nodded.

"An obvious availability," I explained. "Her sex shows. You are a highly attractive girl in your scrubbed, tanned, beach-girl way. But she appeals more to the lovers of the indoor sport."

"You mean she's—more brazen, more obviously vulgar?"

"That isn't what I meant and you know it. Was it because of this pukey Duncan Guest? Is that what started your resentment?"

She inhaled and looked at the bed. "I—suppose. No girl has *ever* before taken a man away from me, not a man I wanted."

"Well, it will probably happen again, so grow up. You're out of high school, Red. You're all alone in the crummiest section of a real crummy town. And don't let Sergeant Macrae's promise lower your guard. You tell your friend in the Santa Monica Department what happened today. They've got lots of extra cops."

"But no jurisdiction here."

"You tell him. Let him worry about jurisdiction."

She sipped her drink and said nothing. I sipped mine and said the same. It was quiet, peaceful and the air was delicately fragrant with her perfume. Perhaps it came from the open bed.

"You think I'm a damned *baby*," she said suddenly.

"I think maybe you were before you met Duncan Guest. That should bring a woman to maturity fast."

Her chin quivered. We went back to silence. I had a doubtful hope that some revelation might be born of the recent violence and our current empathy. I sat and waited, looking benign.

She said finally, "It's four-thirty. I've a dinner date at six."

"I'll go," I told her, "as soon as I finish this drink."

"I—didn't mean that."

"I'll go anyway. Is there anything you want to tell me now that you had reason to withhold before?"

She looked at me candidly and shook her head.

"I'll check with you from time to time. Okay?"

"I'd appreciate it," she said. "You're—all right, Mr. Puma."

I stood up and finished my drink. "Thank you. Is the dinner date with Einar Hansen?"

She frowned. "No. What made you ask that?"

"Nothing. It was a throwaway line. Keep your chin up, Red."

"Check with me from time to time, like you promised."

I went over and kissed her on the forehead. I said, "Natch." I left her smiling.

I drove over to the Venice Station. Petalious was on the way in but they had had no luck with my adversaries. The license plates on the Lincoln had been stolen plates.

I was going past the hamburger stand when I saw the sign was off the door. I parked next to the Tennis Club and walked over.

Einar was at one end of the counter, reading a *Mirror-News*.

"How was the funeral?" I asked.

"Jammed. He sure had a lot of friends, that guy."

And at least one enemy, I thought. I asked, "Got anything besides hamburgers and hot dogs?"

He folded the paper. "I could fix you some shrimp."

"Got beer?"

He nodded. "In bottles. That's what you want, shrimp and beer." He went to the refrigerator. "Ever see those hoodlums again?"

"About an hour ago. They worked me over."

He turned to stare at me. "No kidding?"

I didn't answer. I reached for the *Mirror-News*.

"They were just stooges," he said. "Who do you think sicked 'em on you?"

"My best guess would be Mike Petalious."

He turned on the deep fryer and went over to get me a glass of water. He put it in front of me and stood looking out at the ocean.

I said, "What kind of girl is that Sheila Gallegan?"

He shrugged. "She's okay. Kind of—argumentative. I get a feeling she's fighting herself all the time. She had a case on Dunk for a while."

"So did Deborah Huntington—for a while."

"Huh!" he said. "And still. You should have seen her at the funeral."

"Did she cry?"

"No, it was worse than that. She wanted to cry but couldn't. She looked like she was going to break into little pieces."

"You sound like a gossip columnist," I said. "How could you guess what she was feeling?"

He shook his head. "You should have seen her. Man, she was like a babe walking a tight wire. That Dunk— he hooked 'em. They were thinking about marriage, man."

"Come off it," I said. "Maybe he was, because of the money, but she's over him already."

"Huh!" he said again. "You didn't know Duncan Guest, mister."

"My name," I told him, "isn't 'man' or 'mister.' It's Joe Puma. You can remember a little thing like that, can't you?"

He turned to stare at me. "What are you hot about?"

"I'm sick of hearing about Duncan Guest and his conquests. I'm fed up with the man. He's shaping up as scum in my mind."

Einar Hansen looked at me pityingly. "He's dead, dead, dead. Who can hate the dead?"

"I can. Isn't that fryer hot enough yet?"

"Not yet. There are other restaurants."

"I like this one," I said, "because of the courteous service." I began to read the *Mirror-News*, ignoring him.

The shrimp was excellent and the beer was cold. I
finished both and ordered another bottle of beer. With
the whiskey I'd had, the beer was getting to me a little,
but that was all right. I wanted some edges blurred.

Two muscle men in swimming trunks came in and
sat at the far end of the counter. They ordered hamburgers and malts. They ate and talked about Duncan
Guest. Hansen went down to their end of the counter.

I checked the menu for prices and had the exact
amount without any need for change. I put it on the
counter and went out without saying good-bye.

I was at a temporary dead end. Until I heard from
Curt Huntington or there was a move from the other
side, I had no new avenues to investigate. I drove carefully to the office. My vision was hazy and I felt weak;
I was getting a reaction finally from the violence and
the whiskey, beer and shrimp.

In the washroom down the hall, I bathed my face
in cool water and washed my hands. It was six o'clock
and the traffic in the street below was continuous and
murderous. I sat and thought and nothing bright came
to me.

I called my phone-answering service and was informed that a Miss Huntington had phoned at three-
thirty and was expecting a return call.

I didn't want to phone her, but she was my client.

"I'm lonely," she said. "I'm blue."

"So am I. Did your brother find out what I asked him
to?"

"I've no idea. What'd you ask him to find out?"

"The name of a man. I saw Miss Gallegan this afternoon. She told me you were the one who took Duncan
Guest away from her."

"I'm surprised she'd admit it."

"I'm surprised you didn't tell me the same thing. All
these things are important, Deborah. I can't work in the
dark."

"The hell you can't. *Let's not fight!*"

"All right. I'm sorry that you're lonely and blue.
Couldn't Gregory Harvest do something about that?"

"Greg? That square? Have you been talking to him?"

"He's been threatening me. He told me he was very
fond of you and I should watch my step. I certainly

wouldn't want to get on the wrong side of a big-shot lawyer like that."

She chuckled. "Aren't you the humble one? I could make him a small-shot lawyer with a flick of the wrist. My God, you're not impressed by Greg Harvest, are you?"

"Because of my background," I assured her, "money has always impressed me. And because of my trade, I've learned to stay on the right side of City Hall. Which is just another name for money."

"Aren't we depressed today?" she said jeeringly. "What you need is a good dose of Alden Poltice. He's at The Elms."

"He's a very funny man," I agreed, "but I can't afford The Elms."

"I can."

"Lucky you," I said. "Well, tell your brother to phone me the minute he gets that name."

"Wait—" she said. "Joe, I need a friend. Tonight, just tonight. I'm not going to crowd you, but I need somebody strong and arrogant around tonight."

"I'm not feeling so well," I told her. "I was worked over this afternoon in that lot below Sheila Gallegan's apartment. It should make the late papers. You can read about it there."

A silence. "Joe—"

"That's right. I was sapped and then kicked around. Miss Gallegan nursed me back to health."

A longer silence. "I want to hear about it. It's important that I do. As your client, I order you to take me to The Elms tonight on the expense account and tell me all about your day. That's where I want to get your report, at The Elms."

Why fight it? It was her money. I said, "I'll go home and shower and get on the old blue suit. I'll pick you up at nine."

"I thought we could have dinner there."

"I've already had dinner at Einar Hansen's hamburger stand. I'll pick you up at nine. You'd better phone for the reservation; my name doesn't really send them at The Elms."

"Yes, dear," she said softly. "Yes, lover."

She was a dandy. I would hate to be her psychiatrist. I went home and showered. I put on a heavy robe and set the alarm for eight-fifteen. It was now a little after seven and an hour's nap might help. I flopped on the bed.

They all went around in my mind and made me dizzy, all of them from Adonis to Sheila Gallegan. I thought about the funeral and for some reason that led me to thinking about Mike Petalious' woman, but I couldn't see any connection.

Finally I dozed off.

SEVEN

THE MAITRE D' at The Elms smiled warmly at Deborah, glanced casually at me and said pointedly, "This way, Miss Huntington."

I went along. I'd brung her. I resisted the impulse to backhand the suave son-of-a-bitch and walked quietly in their wake, trying to look like I was at home here.

Einar's, that was my kind of joint. But even Einar hadn't been as courteous to me as I'd expected this afternoon.

Our present host held Deborah's chair as a waiter sidled in to handle mine, and we were seated efficiently and quietly in a nook that afforded a fine view of the floor but also managed a medium of privacy.

The maitre d' smiled at me bleakly. "Is this satisfactory, sir?"

"Dandy," I said. "Your toupee's on crooked."

A momentary horror came to his face and he started to reach a hand toward his hair.

"April fool," I said.

He went away stiffly and Deborah looked at me sadly. "High school fullback at his first party. Adolescent."

"Yes'm. I don't like to be patronized by servants."

"You and Sheila Gallegan," she said. "You two are your own worst enemies."

"Possibly. Neither of us has been driven to a head-shrinker's couch, yet, though."

She colored and looked away.

I said quickly, "I apologize. That was a cruel and stupid thing to say and I wish you were a man so you could hit me for it."

"I'll think of something," she promised. "Do you want anything to eat?"

"I could use a sandwich. How about you?"

"Cold turkey," she said. "I phoned Greg this time, to break the date."

I frowned. "You mean you had a date with him to-night, too?"

She nodded, studying me.

I said, "Greg has sent me quite a lot of work in the past. You fixed me."

"I have a number of friends," she said, "who occa-sionally have need of a man of your unique talents. They'll more than make up any losses you'll suffer through Gregory Harvest."

"You said you were lonely," I reminded her "and now I learn you already had a date when you told me that."

"Being with Greg can be lonelier. We're fighting again, Joe."

I ordered a pair of turkey sandwiches and coffee. We had finished that and were working on some whiskey sours when Greg Harvest came in. There was a blonde with him, a girl in a white sheath dress and a mink stole.

I looked over to find Deborah watching me. I said, "The mink would be cerulean, I suppose. And you staged this, didn't you?"

Her stare was perplexed. "Are you crazy? Staged what?"

"Greg bringing the blonde, dressed like that. A little trick you two cooked up to heckle me."

"Greg . . . ?" She looked around the room and saw him. She took a deep breath and looked back at me. "I swear to you I had nothing to do with Greg and his girl."

"Murder is nothing to base a gag on," I said.

"Of course not. How monstrous do you think I am? Damn you, Joe Puma, apologize!"

"I apologize," I said quietly. "But I'll bet it was his idea of a gag. Is that the shade of mink that's called cerulean?"

She nodded. "It's cerulean. He's coming over."

I turned to see him heading our way. He had left the blonde at the table. His cherubic face was genial and his curly hair looked as though it had just been washed. The All-American boy.

"Well, well," he said jovially. "Business, I hope?"

I nodded. Deborah asked, "Who's the blonde?"

"Isn't she striking? She's a model for Regal Furs. Certainly you're not jealous, Deb?"

"A little," she said. "You mean a lot to me, Greg. And I mean a lot to you, don't I? Thousands."

His face stiffened.

I asked him, "A gag, Greg? If it is, it's in horrible taste."

He looked at me blankly. "Gag—?"

"The white sheath dress and the cerulean mink stole," I explained. "Was that all for me? Or perhaps a publicity gag?"

I thought I saw sudden perspiration on his forehead. He said earnestly, "Believe me, I never even thought of it. My God, it's not that uncommon a combination."

There was a moment of embarrassed silence all around. Then Deborah said, "I guess we—jumped to the wrong conclusion, Greg. It was nice seeing you."

That last sentence had been a clear dismissal. He stared at her sickly and glared at me. He mumbled something and went back to his table.

"Doesn't it give you a wonderful sense of power?" I asked her.

She didn't answer. She looked past me at the blonde and sipped her drink.

And then Alden Poltice came on and he was good for both of us. He had an off-beat sense of humor, never vulgar, occasionally beyond me, timely, satirical and beautifully venomous.

When he had finished, I was almost human again, and the well-washed and delicately perfumed people around me looked human, too. That was what the world needed, more humorists and fewer nuclear physicists.

I had told Deborah about my losing fight on the drive over. I had told her everything else I had learned today. There was no reason for us to prolong the evening.

I asked, "Ready to go?"

"Aren't we going to dance?"

"On that postage stamp floor? When I dance, I want room. The Palladium, that's my kind of floor."

"Let's go," she suggested. "I've never been there."

"Of course you haven't. That's for common people. It's a dance hall, Deborah."

"I know what it is," she said. "Les Green is there. Please, Joe?"

So that's where we went, to the workingman's Ciro's, and Les Green had never been better and Deborah danced like a dream and for a few hours I could almost believe it was just another enjoyable Saturday night with one of my girls, this one a little more attractive than the rest.

What was left of the illusion died as I drove her up past the Lombardy poplars to the front door. The maid was there to open the door, and I said good-night without kissing her, and she told me gravely that she had *never* had a better time and couldn't I come for dinner tomorrow? They usually ate Sunday dinner around four o'clock.

I hesitated, hating to be rude.

"Forget your terrible pride and your inverse snobbery," she asked softly. "Please, Joe?"

"You deserve better company," I said, "but I'll be here."

"Come early," she said. "We can swim. In the morning, if you want to."

"I'll come around one o'clock," I promised. "I'm going to sleep in the morning."

I parked in the garage tonight, and walked along through the open court toward the steps that led to my apartment. There was a woman sitting in the big canvas chair in the court. She was dozing, stirring in her sleep.

It was two-thirty in the morning and I wondered if

she was drunk. There was only one bulb in the court, a small, yellow, insect-repellent light.

She must have heard my steps on the concrete of the court, for she sat up quickly and I saw who it was. It was Mike Petalious' woman.

I walked closer. People were sleeping in the apartments all around us, so I whispered, "Were you waiting for me?"

She whispered back, "That's right. You got Mike in trouble, didn't you? Why?"

"I didn't get him in trouble, Miss Quintana," I said.

"Yes you did, nosing around. You even learned my name, I see. The police are holding Mike. Why? That's what I want to know."

"Ask them," I said, "not me."

"What did he ever do to you? To anybody?"

"He broke Adonis' arm. What does a guy have to do these days to get four duplexes and two triplexes? Whatever it is, Mike did it. And I would bet he sent those two slobs that worked me over, not being man enough to come himself."

"You talk like you hate him," she said. "Why?"

"I don't hate him. Why did you come here? What do you want from me?"

"I want to know what it's all about. Mike and I never had any trouble before. Mike wrestled and the fans loved it and the police weren't interested in us or in wrestling. And now they are. And it started with you, you and Adonis. And Adonis could be cutting his own throat, having the police look into wrestling."

"Anything crooked is going to be looked into from time to time," I said. "It will blow over and you'll have your Mike back. Just sit it out."

"Maybe it won't blow over," she said. "I want to know who's behind you. Everything was comfortable and fun before you came along."

"The law is behind me," I said. "The Los Angeles Police Department. You ask Sergeant Macrae about that."

A window opened somewhere and a feminine voice said, "For heaven's sakes, it's two-thirty in the morning. Can't you find a better place to talk?"

Mike's woman glared at me and I looked at her. I whispered, "Go home and get some sleep. If Mike isn't involved in the murder, he'll be released. There's nothing I can do for you."

She called me something then, but I didn't understand it. It sounded like Spanish and it was probably a good thing I didn't understand Spanish. She stood up, and reached out to slap my face.

"That's right, sister," somebody called. "Don't let him get away with anything. He's got a wife and three kids."

She stalked off through the front of the court, toward the street and I went up to my apartment. Women. . . .

She sits there in that cold court until two-thirty in the morning so she can slap my face. The fat and easy life hadn't been threatened; with two triplexes and four duplexes, did Mike need wrestling any more? What had bothered her?

His being in jail, probably. A Quintana bedded down with a wrestler was bad enough, but now Mike was in the clink and her relatives would read about that. That would make the newspapers. The other things he had done hadn't been in the newspapers, not the wrong things.

I warmed some milk and drank it. My face was still red from where she had slapped me and my ribs were still red from where the hoodlums had kicked me. I was too tired to hate any of them. I went right to sleep.

I got out of bed at ten and looked out the window to see that the overcast was just starting to get burned off by the sun.

I scrambled four eggs with cream, toasted some raisin bread and made a full pot of coffee to go with the Sunday paper. The paper was the *Times.* The *Los Angeles Times.* They do love to compare themselves to *The New York Times* but they are to *The New York Times* what Elmer Kenilstube is to Dizzy Dean. In case you never heard of Elmer Kenilstube, he pitched for Elkville in the Dakota League and set a record, losing sixteen consecutive games.

So a lousy paper, but still the best in this town and the coffee was good. My time wasn't completely wasted. They had increased their total book coverage from one to a generous two pages and it wasn't the football season, so the sport pages were almost readable. During the football season, eighty percent of the sport page coverage is devoted to UCLA and SC and why they are overlooked by the eastern writers.

On the murder, there was nothing I didn't know, except I hadn't known a photographer had taken a picture of me when I was unconscious on that empty lot. There was a picture of Sheila Gallegan crying too, and a statement from Sergeant Macrae that encouraging progress was being made on the case.

Encouraging to whom? The killer?

I turned to the drama section and read about the stars, the feminine stars. I do love to read about them and imagine myself in their lives, dancing and like that. On the stars, the *Times* does an adequate job. *American* stars, I mean, and the skinny Italian ones. Those big Italian stars you can have, all tits and guts.

The sun was completely through the overcast by the time I finished the Sunday paper and the thought of Huntington's pool was pleasant. And some Huntington chow; I didn't have it so bad. She was kind of a star. She'd had some good bits.

Curt Huntington was in the pool when I got there. He was slim but beautifully muscled, tanned and lithe and he swam like a champion. Which I later learned he had been, a collegiate champion.

Deborah in her suit was no surprise; I had seen her in less than that. I could understand why Gregory Harvest could get adolescent about her. All that and money, too; it would be enough of a loss to break the hearts of stronger men than pretty Gregory Harvest.

Like rich people should, we idled the hours away, drinking gimlets, smoking, lolling, swimming, yacking. And being with her like that, against this background, it was hard to believe about her the things a man simply had to believe.

I'd had personal experience with her beyond the hearsay. And I am not young enough to believe that a girl who succumbs too quickly to me hasn't succumbed as quickly dozens of times before.

Well, maybe it wasn't a sin. Who am I to judge? But when it gets to be a compulsion it is sure as hell as much of a degradation as any other compulsion, including overeating.

She had to go to the kitchen to tell the cook something about dinner and her brother said, "I think she's going to be all right, don't you? Duncan was very close to us, and I was afraid she would take his death too hard."

"I think she's going to be all right," I answered.

He took a breath and stared at the still water in the pool. "She's essentially innocent, Deborah is. She's a wonderful girl."

"I'm beginning to get along with her," I said. "She sure as hell can be charming when she wants to be, can't she?"

He nodded. "She doesn't want to be, often. We grew up with some very dull friends and almost any kind of charm is wasted on them." He lighted a cigarette. "She likes you. She likes you a lot."

"Don't worry about it," I said. "I know my place."

"I like you, too," he said, "and I can make you a new place any time you ask me to. You'd be good for Deborah."

"Whoa!" I said. "Back up, Mr. Huntington. Jesus, this isn't my league at all."

"You underrate yourself," he said mildly. "You're intelligent and more literate than you like to admit, and kind and strong and extremely amiable when you want to be."

I grinned. "All that I admit. But I am also lower middle class and proud of it, and I'm my own man and proud of it. I couldn't ever live on anyone's money but my own."

"You wouldn't have to. You're thinking emotionally, Joe. And that's a bad habit. It has stymied millions of men, men of ability. It's what distinguishes the lions from the lambs."

I stretched out and said nothing. I looked at the big house and the beautiful grounds all around and the bright sky overhead. Had he ever talked like this to Greg Harvest, I wondered?

I said, "That Gregory Harvest certainly carries the torch, doesn't he? He's almost pathetic."

"He's just pathetic enough to frighten me," Curt said, "if you know what I mean."

"I know exactly what you mean, because he scares me, too."

Then Deborah was back and she asked, "Who scares you? This is a man I want to see."

"Mike Petalious," I said. "The man who broke Adonis Devine's arm. His girl friend was waiting for me when I got home last night."

Deborah's voice was cool. "Oh?"

I told them about it, including the remarks from the audience.

Deborah said, "Wasn't she a Quintana?"

"She still is," Curt answered. "Mike hasn't gotten around to marrying her, yet."

"Juanita," Deborah said thoughtfully, "Juanita Quintana. She went to Lindsay Hall. Tall girl."

"Big girl," I said, "but beautifully proportioned. Girl would be the wrong word for her; she's all woman."

"I'm sure you'd know," Deborah said. "It's time to get ready for dinner. We—don't eat in our swimming clothes, Joe."

Curt winked at me and I kept a straight face. "Yes, Miss Huntington. Thank you. I have to be cued in on the mores of the upper classes."

She didn't smile. "How long did she stay?"

"Long enough," I said. "Let's get dressed."

It was absurd. It was like a high school crush. I had known her three days. What kind of compulsion was this? It wasn't as though she needed to grab any man who came along. Even if she hadn't had money, she wouldn't have to push. She had the figure, the face, the charm, the lure. Add a few millions to that, and what would she need Joe Puma for?

Not that I'm repulsive, but even at the Palladium I had never made out like this. Of course, at the Palladium, they don't care if you're big and strong and arrogant. Those skinny, little, smooth guys make out even better at the Palladium.

Juanita Quintana. . . . Had she found the Lindsay Hall girls dull, too? And the rest of her childhood friends? What did Mike Petalious have that her friends had lacked? I had known a number of rich people and a distressing majority of them were dull, but so were most middle and lower class citizens. If you have to be bored, money would be more help than hindrance, I

should think. I'd be· willing to try it, anyway. If you
can afford good booze, who can bore you?

Dinner was guinea hen and wild rice; the salad dressing had a number of ingredients I couldn't identify and
the salad itself had two, but it was all heavenly.

We were on the cognac when Curt was called to the
telephone. He came back to tell me, "I've got the name
you asked me to get for you now—Arnold Giampolo.
Recognize it?"

"Vaguely. Owned a couple fighters, didn't he?"

Curt smiled. "And a few oil wells and some buildings
downtown."

"Did you get an address?"

He smiled, and handed me a slip of paper. "It's all
there, courtesy of Attorney Gregory Harvest."

"And where did he get it?"

"He didn't say. I can call him back and ask him, if
you want."

"No. I guess it isn't important. I can always ask him
later, in case this Giampolo plays it dumb."

"Tell me," Curt said wonderingly, "what do you do
when you go up against a man of that stature? You
certainly can't walk in cold and call him a crook."

"I'll have to feel my way," I answered. "To tell you
the truth, it will be the first time I went up against a
man that big. Financially, I mean. I'll just have to fish
and wait for a reaction."

Curt said, "The reaction could be delayed and violent,
too, couldn't it?"

I nodded. "That's my only excuse for charging a hundred dollars a day. On an efficiency basis, I'd never get
that much."

He didn't say any more about that. They couldn't
understand a job like mine, and I have friends who feel
the same way about it. The whole profession has a bad
smell to outsiders and it's loaded with discredited cops
and seniority-soured FBI men.

Greg Harvest came after dinner and some other people,
and it gave me an excuse to leave. Deborah gave me
a little argument about that, but not too much. I had
a feeling she didn't seriously care whether I was there
or not so long as we couldn't be alone.

It had been too pleasant a day to cap with a visit to Arnold Giampolo but it was too early for me to waste the rest of the day in front of a TV set. I drove over to Venice, to a stoolie I knew.

He had been a part of the Bugsy Siegel mob out here until the local law had broken up that combine. He still had a ready ear and a fairly sharp nose when he wasn't sodden with grape, and there was a possibility I could pick up an item or two if he was home.

I bought a bottle of fifty-nine-cent muscatel in a liquor store on the way.

He lived in a lean-to rooming house run by a retired prostitute on a back lot off one of the discarded canals. His name was Snip Caster and he was in his room tonight, playing gin rummy with his landlady.

This retired lady of the evening was about sixty now, ornery, bony and rheumatic. She wasn't happy to see me.

"It was our night, Snip," she said. "What's this wino doing here?"

"He's no wino," Snip informed her. "The grape's for me. Right, Joe."

"Right," I said cheerfully. "And I won't be long, Aggie."

She sniffed. "You'd better not be. I save my Sundays for Snip. He's getting a break." She went out grumbling under her breath.

In his palmier days, Snip had been a glib, brazen and slippery small man. He was now none of these things except small. He was furtive, apologetic, and he lived in the sweet-sour stink of the wino. But his brain had not completely degenerated yet; he had the instinct to pick up any available dollar.

I put the wine on his bureau and asked, "Like to make a few bucks?"

"Always, Joe."

"I know you used to hang around with the wrestlers when Bugsy was operating and I thought you might know something about the operation."

"It's big," he said. "It's bigger than the law thinks."

I nodded. "And who's the biggest man in it?"

"Devine, I suppose. You know, the guy put up the reward for that kill over on Dune Street."

"He's not in the management end, is he? He's a performer."

"He could have a piece of the top, too. I may be way off on that, but it's a thing I think I heard once."

"Could you find out more, maybe?"

Snip shrugged. "I could try. I ain't got the contacts I used to have, you know."

"And another man," I went on, "the guy who runs the hamburger stand next to Muscle Beach—Hansen."

"I washed dishes for him a couple times," Snip said. "A stiff from nothing. Good buddy of the guy got bumped, though. They used to play chess for hours right there on the counter."

"Thanks, Snip. Ten bucks if you find out something really helpful."

"Five in advance, maybe?" he asked meekly. "I owe Aggie three."

I gave him five. I thought of some of the theatrical blondes he had squired when he was a lip for the mob, and it seemed sad to me he should wind up in this dingy room with Aggie. It was probably the finest kind of justice, but did any man deserve *this?*

Patches of fog were drifting in from the ocean as I went out into the subdued revelry of Sunday night on the Speedway. There was a smell of salt air and wine on the slight breeze.

It wasn't on my way home, but I drove past Einar's and saw he was closed and I continued toward Dune Street. There was a light in Sheila Gallegan's apartment and a new Chev sedan parked on the lot. I had a flashlight in the car and a doubtful remembrance of seeing the Chev somewhere before tonight.

His registration, strapped to the steering column, identified the Chev as Einar Hansen's.

Aggie and Snip, Einar and Sheila, Greg and Deborah; everybody was paired up for the evening. Joe Puma drove home alone.

And who should be waiting for me in his big fat Cad convertible but my first client in this business, the beautiful Adonis Devine? He was parked in front of my apartment building.

"Been waiting long?" I asked.

"An hour," he said. "I'd have waited until you got here, no matter how long. It's important I talk to you."

"Financially important?" I guessed.

He looked at me belligerently. "Right. Is that beneath your notice?"

"Hell, no. Come on up."

We went up the steps quietly to my modest dump and I asked him, "Beer, booze, coffee?"

He shook his head and sat in the worn tapestry upholstered chair, staring at the dull wall opposite him.

"Going to withdraw the reward offer?" I asked.

He glanced at me, startled. "Why did you say that?"

"Oh, it shapes up that way. You're at a financial level now where you can no longer afford to be a man's friend."

"You're lippy," he said. "What makes you so sarcastic?"

"My cynicism. You made this big three grand gesture because you were a friend of Duncan Guest's. He had almost made you what you are. And then the smart boys in your dodge pointed out to you that wrestling couldn't stand too much investigation and what you were doing was cutting your own throat. Because if wrestling dies, what are you? I'll tell you—you're Clarence Kutchenreuter, just another refugee from the corn belt."

"Take it easy," he said harshly.

"Take it easy, hell. You don't scare me any more than you scared Mike Petalious. And he doesn't scare me, either, and the guys who are pulling his strings don't scare me. I'm not rich, you see; I've got nothing to lose."

"You got plenty to lose," he said. "You've got your teeth and your health."

"And you had a friend," I said. "Duncan Guest. Remember him?"

"He's dead."

"Sure. The question is—are *you?*"

He didn't answer; glaring at me.

I said, "I asked a lot of people who the biggest man in the wrestling racket is, and they told me Devine. And I heard it was bigger than that; he even had a piece of the top. True?"

"Not yet, it isn't. Who do we hurt? We bill them as exhibitions. That could be anything. A juggling act, a dog act, a crooner. So some of the cruds think it's on the level. Are they hurt? They're soft in the head, sure, but cleaning up wrestling isn't going to make 'em any brighter. Cruds we will always have."

"And wrestling, too," I said. "The police simply aren't interested in disturbing any racket as peaceful as the wrestling farce. I'm working with them to find a killer, not ruin TV's number-one attraction."

"And if it was a Syndicate kill?"

"Somebody will go to jail or the gas chamber," I answered, "and all the smart guys in your line will froth at the mouth publicly and say it is a good thing and what we need is a new look in wrestling and the cruds will get a new look, run by the same old operators. Now, who conned you into thinking I should quit investigating for the good of wrestling?"

He stared at me. "You're sure mouthy. You're as mouthy as Duncan was."

"Who sent you, Adonis?" I persisted. "Or are you the top?"

"I'm not the top. Never mind who sent me. Maybe nobody. Maybe I can think for myself a little and see where the wind's blowing."

"Maybe the moon's Roquefort, too. All right, withdraw your reward. I'm getting paid and I'm continuing to work. Withdraw your reward and be a villain to the cruds. The gate will be the same; they'll come to see you get beat. But you got the looks for a hero, and they maybe won't be able to make the mental adjustment."

"Jesus, you are cynical, aren't you?"

"Not quite enough," I said, "and that keeps me poor. That's why I haven't got a Cad convertible."

He stood up. "I'll talk to you again, okay? I'll keep the reward going for a while."

"It's great publicity," I said. "It makes your hero image bigger than ever."

He stood there, feet well spread, muscular body well balanced, studying me thoughtfully. "I ought to try you out for size. Nobody talks to me the way you do."

"Clarence," I said, "be your age. You're not playing in a jock-strap western now, where the blond always wins. This is the cruel, cruel world and you were brought this far by a smart friend, now dead. You would be making a serious mistake, tangling with me."

"Maybe some day I will," he said quietly. "And maybe find out what I'm beginning to suspect—you're all mouth."

"It's only one of my weapons," I informed him. "Good-night, Adonis."

He left without answering. He went out and I went to the kitchen to make some cocoa. And while I was out there, I scrambled some eggs. That guinea hen didn't stick to the ribs.

He hadn't scared me. Muscle doesn't scare me as much as brains. Muscle I got. Greg Harvest, there was a guy that scared me.

EIGHT

SUNDAY WENT AWAY, as it always does, and Monday came in colder and overcast, gray and smoggy. It murders my eyes, that smog, but it doesn't keep the suckers from coming out in droves to golden sunny Southern California. Los Angeles is where they head for and that's where they stay unless they can find a job somewhere else. Very few of them can find a job somewhere else. So they live in the smog and read about the snow back home and try to feel superior. It isn't easy.

The *Times* had sent the murder to one of the inner pages and that officially made it unimportant news. The front page had the important news: a forty-seven-year-old ingenue was getting a divorce from her fifth husband.

About the murder there was nothing but print to fill space. The police were nowhere, just as Puma was. The sport pages carried last night's wrestling bouts with a straight face, exactly as though they were straight sport news. Nobody had yet thought of transferring them to the entertainment pages. And Adonis had called *me* a cynic.

The roller derby results were there, too, another sport turned into a farce by the bright boys. In the fall, the college football games would be reported· as amateur contests between students. That was the most lamentable tragedy of all, a really great American sport gone to hell, degraded by the alumni and the sport writers.

Bitter thoughts on a bleak day; what was any of it

to me? I was getting paid and getting laid, eating well
and still breathing the free air, tainted though it was.
I was one million per cent better off than Duncan Guest.
I was even better off than William Shakespeare.

So far as I knew.

I called Sergeant Macrae before I left the house and
learned they had not tracked down the hoodlums
in the Lincoln. Petalious had been released early yesterday morning after admitting nothing and making a
number of derogatory remarks about Joseph Puma. And
what, the Sergeant wanted to know, was new with me?

"Nothing substantial. I had a talk with Devine last
night. He was going to withdraw the reward, but I think
I talked him out of it."

"You must have hopes."

"I wasn't thinking of myself," I lied. "But a reward
like that brings out the informers, doesn't it? It will
help us all."

"It hasn't brought 'em out yet. Well, carry on, Puma."

I got to the office a little before ten and there was
nothing of interest there. I phoned Arnold Giampolo.

A woman answered the phone and I asked for Mr.
Giampolo and she asked me my name and I gave it
to her and she asked me to wait a minute, which I did.

And then a man's voice said, "This is Arnold Giampolo.
Are you the Joe Puma who is a friend of Jack Ross?"

Jack was one of my rich friends, my rich, honest
friends. I said I was the same Joe Puma.

"Investigator, aren't you?" he asked.

"Yes, Mr. Giampolo."

"And what did you want to see me about?"

"About wrestling."

A pause. "You—ah—were thinking about going into
wrestling, Mr. Puma?"

"No. I was hoping to ask you some questions about
it. I understand you control it out here."

A longer pause. "Your information is—unsound. Where
did you get it?"

"In the *World Almanac*, Mr. Giampolo. What difference
does it make if it isn't true?"

"Insolent, too, are you? Jack didn't tell me that."

I said wearily, "I guess I'm wasting your time, sir.
Sorry to have troubled you."

"One moment," he said. "Don't be in a hurry. Nothing can be done right in a hurry. Seriously, I would be interested in learning who told you I was connected with wrestling."

"Duncan Guest did," I lied, "the afternoon of the day he died."

This third pause was the longest of all. Then Giampolo said thoughtfully, "Perhaps you had better come to my house and we'll talk about it. Do you know where I live?"

"Yes, sir," I said. "Guest gave me your address when he gave me your unlisted phone number.

"I see," he said quietly. "I see. I'll be waiting here."

The lie I'd voiced about Duncan Guest could easily have been my wedge. It could also backfire if he questioned me too closely about it. My use of the name hadn't scared him off and yet he must have read about Guest in the papers, even if he didn't know him. It seemed logical to guess he knew him.

The house was old and colonial, two stories of glistening white, with a mammoth pillared porch and red brick chimneys, right out of an MGM set for a deep south epic.

The butler was an aged Negro, natch, and he led me to a circular, covered patio in the rear. Here, a fairly short, thick and broad man was sitting in wash slacks and T-shirt, looking out at his informal gardens. He had a tall drink on the table next to him.

Arnold Giampolo, paisan, making like a colonel from Kentucky. There was a chair next to him, and he nodded toward it, and I took it. He didn't offer his hand.

He didn't even look at me as he said, "I think you lied about Duncan Guest."

I said nothing.

He glanced at me. "Didn't you?"

I shook my head.

"Who sent you to Mike Petalious?"

"Guest."

"Now I know you're lying. Adonis told you about Mike. He admitted that to some friends of mine."

"Two friends in a Lincoln with stolen license plates?" I asked.

"You shouldn't have come here with lies," he said.

I kept my voice calm. "All right, paisan, we'll play a game called honesty. You tell me all your business and I'll tell you all of mine."

He swung his chair around to face mine. He had a round face and short, gray hair and really impressive shoulders. He exuded an aura of power.

"You're not running down some poor hotel skipper, now, Puma. You're playing with people you don't impress."

"I usually am, Mr. Giampolo. And also with people who resent my nosing into their business. But you suggested I come up here; I didn't force my way in. If you have something besides advice to give me, I'm waiting for it."

He studied me quietly. He sipped his drink and looked out at his colorful garden. His voice was almost amiable. "Wrestling is an entertainment medium. The sport in recent years has become profitable for all its participants, chiefly because it has been well promoted and well managed." He sipped his drink again. "There was a certain trashy element in it that has been eliminated, and the sport has been kept clear of the violent and unsavory men who have invaded boxing and tried to invade the collegiate sports."

"It's still crooked," I said, "but that doesn't concern me. Duncan Guest's death is all I'm concerned with."

"I'm sure his death had nothing to do with wrestling."

"I'm not. And I'm not sure you're sure. Wouldn't you call those two hoodlums in the Lincoln violent men?"

He didn't answer.

"You accuse me of lying," I said, "and then give me a song and dance an idiot would gag on. You're not talking to a Rotary luncheon, Mr. Giampolo. I came here for information."

"And I gave it to you. Those men you spoke of are also looking for Duncan Guest's murderer. Wrestling can't afford any murders, Mr. Puma. The two men you dislike may have acted improperly, but only because they were as concerned with the murder as you are. And they may have mistakenly assumed you were working to hide the killer, not find him."

I used a word I'd rather not put in print. It's a product of the horse.

He glared at me.

I said, "If you're so concerned with keeping wrestling clean, you'd turn those two men over to the police. The police are looking for them."

He was quiet a moment. "If they should—voluntarily surrender themselves to the police, would you transfer your quest to another line of investigation?"

"I can't promise anything like that. I have to go where my nose leads me. I hope it leads me back to them and I hope it leads me to them one at a time. That way, we can wind up even."

"Muscle," he said. "All muscle and no brains. Ross was wrong about you."

I said nothing.

"Do the police have my name?" he asked. "You're working with the Los Angeles Police Department, aren't you?"

"I'm working with them but not for them. They won't need to get your name from me unless you're involved in the murder. I make it a rule never to antagonize wealthy people without reason."

"All right," he said, "I'll give you this much then, for your consideration. That hamburger stand proprietor, that Einar Hansen, could be the big key to your puzzle. He was very close to Duncan Guest."

"Do you know any more than that about him?"

Giampolo shook his head. "But I've put together what I do know about the murder, and that's the way it shapes up."

"Nothing else you want to tell me?"

He shook his head.

I stood up. "Well, thanks. Sorry if I was unduly belligerent."

He smiled slightly. "An inherited trait, no doubt. Some day, under kinder circumstances, you'll have to come over for a real Italian dinner. I have the best Italian cook west of New York."

"I'll look forward to it," I said. "I can find my way out."

It had probably been a wasted trip. Except that I had learned he was a big man in the wrestling racket. His advice about Einar Hansen could be sound or could be an attempted red herring. He wasn't a man motivated

by anything beyond self-interest and lies were meaning-
less to him; he lived a lie.

I had no focus in this search, no theory to be sub-
stantiated beyond the persistent intuition that Duncan
Guest's death had been connected with his trade. And
then the thought came to me that I was overlooking
something at the Dune Street place.

It didn't seem likely that the police had overlooked
it but they didn't always confide in me completely. I
headed the Plymouth that way.

How could Sheila Gallegan know the color of the
stole? I hadn't remembered any light over that runway.
Any reflected light from a window would pick up the
white sheath dress, but the subdued color of fur would
require more illumination.

Her old Chev was parked on the lot and I pulled up
next to it. I went up and walked the runway from end
to end. Not a light anywhere. I went back to knock on
the door of Miss Gallegan's apartment.

No answer. Her Chev was below, but she was probably
at the beach. And then I remembered I still had Hansen's
key to Guest's hide-out. And I had never looked at the
scene of the crime, as the newspapers love to call it.

I went down the runway and started to put the key
in the door when someone from within called, "It's not
locked. Come in."

I went in to find Greg Harvest piling clothes on the
bed.

"Ghoul," I said. "They aren't even your size, are
they?"

He looked at me annoyedly. "I'm his attorney. I'm
in charge of his estate."

"You'll wind up with some well-dressed relatives, won't
you?"

He straightened. "Puma, get out of my hair. A man
can take only so much of your kind of lip."

I looked around the place. The furniture was about
the same as Sheila's and was probably included in the
rent. I went into the kitchen and poured myself a glass
of water. From there, I said, "I didn't notice your car
down below."

"It's on a parking lot, a block away, an *attended*
parking lot. I didn't think I should take a chance on it

below. Those wire wheels cost money, you know."

I looked into the refrigerator and saw a quarter pound of rancid butter and some soured milk. Somebody had disconnected the refrigerator.

Greg came out to pour himself a glass of water.

I said, "Talked to Giampolo this morning. He wanted to know who gave me his name."

"Ah?"

"I told him Duncan Guest had, before he died. He said that was probably a lie."

"Don't get too rough with him, Puma."

"I don't intend to." I turned to face him. "Do you want to give me the name of that girl who was with you at The Elms Saturday night?"

"Why? You're reaching, Joe."

"Maybe. Are you in with Giampolo, Greg? Do you have a piece of management in that racket, too?"

"For Christ's sake," he said, "if I was in with him, would I hand you his name?"

"Maybe. I don't know how you complicated guys operate. Maybe it's the right time to cross your partner. Maybe he'd be a good man to throw to a grand jury if wrestling is ever investigated."

He filled another glass of water and sipped it. "Man, you are way out in left field, aren't you? I suppose Guest was the third partner and I killed him?"

"Very interesting theory," I said. "Do you want to give me the name of the blonde, now?"

He sipped the water for a few seconds and then set it on the drainboard. He took a notebook from his pocket, riffed through it, and finally tore out a page.

"I'll not only give you her name; I'll give you the blonde. Very dull girl." He nodded toward the other room. "I don't suppose you'd want to help me carry some of that stuff to the car."

"Gee, I'd like to, Greg," I apologized, "but I'm so damned busy."

He muttered something and went out. He took an armful and went out to the runway and I went to the phone. There was a dial tone; it was still operating.

I phoned Macrae and he was at the station. I gave him the girl's name and address and the circumstances

of my seeing her and told him Harvest was here now,
and did he know it?

"Yes, he checked in here first. This girl looks like a
waste of time to me, Joe."

"If you've got something hotter, ignore her. According
to what I read in the papers, you're where I am—
nowhere."

"All right, all right. What have you been doing this
morning?"

"Nothing much. I got up late. Guest had a lot of
clothes here, didn't he, considering it wasn't his real
home?"

"He had four times as much in his real home. The
way I understand it, he'd quite often stay there for a
few days at a time."

"Adonis didn't tell me that. Why was Adonis worried,
then?"

"Yes. And wouldn't that be a good line of investigation?
Did you know Adonis had gone through a long siege of
psychiatric treatment?"

"Of course, Sergeant. *Everybody* knows that."

"And he was your first client. Maybe we don't know
more than you do, Joe, but we know more than you
want us to."

"Right, Sergeant. I look silly in sheath dresses, though.
I haven't the hips for them. Harvest—there's a guy you
could give some time to. You boys are inclined to under-
estimate the chicanery of lawyers."

From the doorway, Harvest said, "Who the hell are
you talking to?"

"See you later, doctor," I said to Macrae. "I'll take
them every two hours, then. Both of them? Okay." I
hung up. I looked at Greg's shoes and said, "Crepe soles,
eh? Quiet, aren't they?"

"I asked you a question," he said.

"I was talking to my doctor. Those hoodlums kind
of upset my stomach, kicking me there."

He stood quietly, staring at me. I felt an unreasonable
chill. He said, "You were talking about lawyers."

"We always do. His brother-in-law is a lawyer. He
makes more money than Doc and it burns him. His
wife rags him about it."

"You're lying," he said, "as usual." He went over to the bed. "You put the police on Arnold Giampolo and you are going to be in very serious trouble. You'll need more than a lawyer to get you out of it."

"Couldn't you have sent one of your lackeys to pick up those clothes?" I asked. "It looks chintzy for a man of your stature to be walking up this cheap street with an armfull of second-hand clothes."

He stood quietly, studying me. He was breathing hard and his eyes locked mine. "I think," he said finally, "the time has come." He started to take off his jacket.

"Don't be hasty, Greg," I said. "Let's shake hands. Why get all marked up, just because you don't like my lip?"

He paused, his coat half off. "Chicken?" he asked softly.

"Not exactly," I said. "I just want to show you my grip."

He shrugged back into his coat. I held out a hand. He stared at it for seconds and then reached out to grip it.

"The stadium is empty," I said, "and the boys with the whistles are on sick leave. The pom-pom girls have lost their pom-poms and the boys in the band all have dates, some of them with each other. The time has come, All-American, for you to stop being a halfback. Go ahead, *squeeze!*"

I let him get high on my hand; I gave him every advantage. And then I tensed my forearm and his knees shook. I gave it a little more and his face went white and he reached out for my face with his left hand, reached out like a woman would, fingernails first.

I squeezed harder and he went to his knees and a harsh, half-choked sob came from him and his eyes were wet. I felt something crack in his hand, probably one of the small bones, and I released him.

He was on his knees, head forward, whimpering. He was a long way from the Notre Dame game at the moment, back with his mother. I went out quickly, ashamed of myself, sick of myself.

He was smarter than I was and had achieved more. He dressed better, thought better and smelled better. There was no point in my trying to rationalize it. He hadn't deserved that; I had goaded him into it. Because I resented his clear superiority.

But it wasn't the right time to apologize and I couldn't go back now.

NINE

FROM A DRUGSTORE, I phoned my phone-answering service and was informed that a Mr. Snip Caster had called and would await a return call. He could be reached at the number the girl gave me.

The number wasn't Aggie's but I had a hunch whose it was, and I looked up Fat Emil's Bar and Grill and sure enough it was Fat Emil's. It was only a few blocks from where I was.

It was an old stucco building wedged between an Armenian grocery and a Mexican restaurant. It smelled of Lysol and wine, of stale beer and unwashed bodies. A thin man in dirt-glazed overalls was at the bar. Two other men sat at a table near the entrance to the washroom. The bartender looked at me and nodded toward a door in the back of the room.

In this smaller room, Snip Caster was drunkenly asleep and snoring on a canvas army cot. There was a piece of paper in one clenched hand and I took it. I read:

> *One of the men who beat you up, Jake Koski, lives at 3116 Selwin. He was bragging about it last night.*

I didn't put any money into his still clenched hand; it would be stolen for sure. I could always bring it around later. I drove over to Selwin, which is in Playa del Rey.

I passed Harvest, in his Jaguar, on the way over. We were both stopped for a light, facing each other, and I kept my eyes on the light. If I had wanted an excuse to expend some of the animosity bubbling in me, Snip had given me a target. But I had wasted it on Greg, and

Koski would he spared. There would be no physical violence; I was armed.

Number 3116 Selwin was a four-unit building, hidden from the water by the cliff behind it and there was a blue Lincoln convertible parked in front. I didn't remember all of the old number, but I remembered there had been a "Z" in it. There was no "Z" in this number.

They could be another pair of stolen plates, but I doubted it. It's a fool's play, except for short stretches when necessary for a job. I wrote the new number into my notebook and went up the walk to the apartment house.

Three of the mailboxes had names on, but none of the names was Koski. Like Duncan Guest, these gentlemen weren't advertising their residence. The unnamed apartment was #2, to the right on the first floor.

I heard the two-tone chime ring and then a woman's voice and wondered if I had made a mistake. But it was Light-brown who opened the door.

He looked at me and smiled. Without turning around, he said to someone behind him, "It's the wop. What do I do?"

"Bring him in," a voice said. "I want to see the bandages."

Light-brown smiled some more. "Afraid to come in?"

I shook my head. "I talked with Giampolo this morning. He offered me you two for the law, but I turned him down."

The light-brown eyes were suddenly alert and his face momentarily slack in surprise. From behind him, the voice said, "For Christ's sake, bring him in. Let's see what's cooking. Get him out of the hall."

I came into a room of mail-order furniture, of cotton wall-to-wall carpeting and sleazy drapes on traverse rods. Dark-brown sat on a new maple davenport. A chalk-faced blonde with stocky legs and an impressive bust stood in the archway to the dinette.

Dark-brown said to her, "Now would be a good time for you to go to the store. Take the car if you want."

"No rough-house in here," she warned quietly. "I got the place the way I want it, finally, and I won't take no rough-house."

Dark-brown turned to look at her, saying nothing.

"God damn it," she said, "it ain't even paid for yet."

He continued to look at her silently and she went away, toward the kitchen. He looked at me, "What was that name you used outside?"

"Giampolo. Hasn't he called you?"

He shook his head. "Did he call you? Where'd you hear about him?"

"It doesn't matter. Call him; ask him if I didn't talk to him."

He shook his head again. "You said something else out there, about him offering you us."

"That's correct. If I'd lay off the investigation, or at least steer clear of wrestling."

Light-brown came around me to go over and sit next to his partner. The kitchen door slammed.

Dark-brown said, "You sure ain't short on guts."

"Nor muscle," I said. "I'd have taken you both, if you hadn't pulled the sap."

Light-brown muttered something and Dark-brown said, "Shut up, Jake." He continued to stare at me.

I said, "I told Giampolo I couldn't make the deal. I told him I wasn't interested in the crookedness of wrestling, only in the death of Duncan Guest."

"And he gave you this address?"

"No."

"Who, then?"

"It doesn't make any difference," I said. "Here I am."

Dark-brown turned to look at his partner. "You and your big mouth. I wish your brain was as big as your mouth."

"I'm looking for the murderer of Duncan Guest," I said. "Are you?"

He nodded toward a maple chair, upholstered in chintz. "Sit down. You want a beer?"

"I guess." I sat down.

Dark-brown said to his partner, "Get three cans."

Light-brown went to the kitchen and Dark-brown said, "Mr. Giampolo didn't call the play on you; that was our idea. We was to watch you, try to scare you but not lay a hand on you. Mr. Giampolo don't play it heavy."

"That's why he's rich," I said, "and your wife has to settle for mail-order furniture."

He shook his head vexedly. "Boy, you really hunt trouble. You sick or something?" He tapped his temple questioningly.

"Look who's talking. Did I start the fight?"

"Okay, okay. So that was just business. We played it wrong, but it was business. And that broad ain't my wife."

Light-brown came in with three punched cans of beer and handed them around. I lifted mine. "To better understanding."

We all drank.

Dark-brown said, "So what have you got?"

"Practically nothing. How about you?"

He looked at his can of beer. "The guy we're watching now is Einar. But we lost him. He ain't at the stand and he ain't home and we don't know where the hell he is."

A silence, and he asked, "Do you?"

"No. What makes Einar Hansen so interesting?"

"Sorting 'em all over, he was Guest's best friend. He was a guy Guest told things he didn't tell his other friends. This Einar knows plenty about a lot of things, but he never opens his mouth foolish, only when he thinks it's smart."

"The way to get to a man like that," I explained, "is with money."

"If nothing else works, yeah. But first you try the cheaper angles, to keep the operation cost down. That's smart, too, ain't it?"

I nodded and sipped my beer. Light-brown muttered something again and I looked at him. He held my stare. I transferred it to Dark-brown. "Are you going to try Einar with money, now?"

"If we find him. That Gallegan girl, she's an angle, too. Hansen was over there to see her last night. Would you know why?"

"He's a man; she's an attractive girl. Why not?"

"It could be more than that, too. He dated her before and then she put the freeze on him. Last night he's back and stays two hours. Why? Trying to get her real story, I'd say."

"You boys have been busy, haven't you?" I said admiringly. "How'd you learn all that?"

"From friends."

"Wrestlers?"

Again, Koski muttered something. Dark-brown said, "Why not? They saw Hansen every day. They know him. That don't make the kill a wrestling kill, does it?"

"No," I admitted, "but if it isn't a wrestling kill, would you mind telling me why you're interested in it?"

"To find out," Dark-brown said reasonably. "If it is, to protect who we got to protect, and if it isn't, to be sure the police find that out before they go nosing into wrestling. Now, does that make sense to you?"

"Yes," I said. I finished my beer and stood up. "Take it easy around that Gallegan girl. I know I said that before but it's important enough to repeat."

Dark-brown didn't answer. Koski said, "Don't tell us what to do."

I looked at him. "I'm telling you. Do you want to go out in the back yard with me and without your buddy and we'll thresh it out?"

"Any time," he said.

I nodded toward the back of the apartment. "Let's go."

"Relax," Dark-brown said. "You shut up, Jake. He'd eat you, stupid. And Mr. Giampolo would dump you. And you could go back to picking up towels in the locker room."

Koski stood rigidly quiet, looking at nobody.

I said, "I know his name, but I never did catch yours."

"Just call me trouble," Dark-brown said. "That's what my ma always called me."

"Okay, Trouble. See you around, I suppose." I went to the doorway, conscious of their eyes on my back. I went out without looking around.

It was after lunchtime and I was hungry. I went to Smoky Joe's in Santa Monica and ordered a plate of ribs. I phoned Sergeant Macrae from there. He wasn't in, but his partner was.

I told him, "One of the men who beat me up is named Jake Koski and he and his partner are right now in Apartment #2 at 3116 Selwin in Playa del Rey. There's a woman with them."

"Thanks, Puma. I'm surprised you didn't go over there with a baseball bat."

"I'm not physical," I told him. "I'm mental."

"In the worst way," he added. "Keep your nose clean."

I sat down to my ribs feeling more like a citizen. Not giving them Giampolo had bothered me and I had partially repaid my conscience by giving them the hoodlums. Giampolo was too rich for me to toy with; unless he became more involved than he presently was, perhaps I would never need to reveal him.

Who's perfect? Are you?

Two Santa Monica uniformed officers came in and sat at the counter. The older one of the pair looked at me frowningly a moment before sitting down. I concentrated on my food, feeling like Mickey Cohen must feel in Beverly Hills.

The older one leaned over toward the younger one at the counter and the younger one looked at me. I looked back at him without interest. He turned away and they both laughed quietly.

Resentment bubbled in me and I fought it. I had already made an unmitigated ass of myself once today. Once a day is enough, too much. They had their pensions and their uniformed arrogance but also their hungry families and the dislike of practically everybody they met.

Who's perfect? I asked myself. Am I?

I finished the ribs and gulped my coffee and left Smoky Joe's.

There wasn't much point to it, but I drove over to the Petalious duplex. A Cadillac Coupe de Ville was parked in front of the place. I walked to the rear half of the establishment and rang the bell.

Mike came to the door. He glowered at me and asked, "Come to tangle, tough guy?"

"It wouldn't be fair unless you're armed," I said casually. "Because I am."

"I could break your arm before you got your gun out," he said.

"Possibly," I admitted. "But I can shoot with either hand. I thought we could talk, Mike."

He shook his head stubbornly.

"Phone your boss," I suggested. "Ask him if it's all right to talk with me."

He studied me warily. "Who's my boss?"

"I know. Maybe you don't, so I won't voice the name. But if you do, phone him."

"You don't know nothing," he said. "You're fishing. Get out of here. It's my property. Beat it."

I shrugged and turned away. The door slammed behind me.

I was down to the sidewalk when I saw Miss Quintana coming from the north, a bag of groceries in one arm. She was wearing a sweater and skirt and she walked erectly and gracefully, doing both articles of apparel full justice. A woman who was all woman. I waited.

"Can't you leave him alone?" she asked me. "He isn't bothering you. Can't you get off his back?"

"I'll try. Married yet?"

"You're no gentleman, are you?"

"I'm a peasant," I agreed. "Great melting pot, this America. Remember me to all the girls at Lindsay Hall."

Her fine body stiffened and her eyes glowed hotly. "You're not only insolent, you're cruel. Mike is twice the man you are."

I shook my head and stared at her. How could she say that? Sharp, personable, handsome guy like me. She was blind. What did that Greek have that I didn't have? In the order of their importance: two triplexes, four duplexes and a Cadillac Coupe de Ville. But she didn't need these, a Quintana.

There was no understanding women. At the Palladium, there had been a lanky, skinny guy with a real girlish face who did better than I did, night after night, when that was my stamping grounds. Women are absurd.

She stared at me and I stared at her and I had the strange feeling that she could be measuring me as I was her, she could be seeing me as I tried to imagine her, under the sweater and skirt.

Then, from the rear unit, a voice called, "What the hell is going on out there? What are you two talking about?"

It was Mike and there had been more than annoyance in his voice. There had been doubt, there had been jealousy.

She flushed, I thought. She looked toward the open doorway and smiled. She called, "I've been telling him you're a better man than he is."

I gave her my most superior smile. There had been challenge in her voice.

"He knows that," Mike called. "Hurry up, I'm hungry."

She stood where she was. Who was he, to order a Quintana around? She looked at me musingly.

And Mike went over the edge. He called hoarsely, "Bring him in here. We'll see who's the best man. We can use the back yard."

The challenge was in her eyes now as she looked at me. "Well, Mr. Puma?"

"Why not?" I said. "It's been a dull day so far."

The back yard served only the rear unit and there was a concrete block wall seven feet high on three sides of it. The house blocked any view from the front.

The grass was clipped short and it was dry. I took off my shoes, my jacket and my socks. I took off my pistol harness and put that with the holster and the gun on a redwood table near the patio. Mike took off his sport shirt and kicked off his loafers.

His chest stretched his T-shirt to the limit and his arms were long and impressive. This was no TV wrestler, flying through the air in the phony tackles and blocks, in the highly vulnerable running head rams. This was a man who knew his trade and he could break my arm without stretching the T-shirt any more than he was right now.

He said grimly, "You can fight any damned way you want to. I'll wrestle straight unless you pull something raw. Then I'll show you how many dirty tricks even the decent wrestlers know."

"I always fight any damned way I want to," I told him. "You do the same."

From the redwood bench next to the redwood table, Miss Quintana watched with anticipation and obvious pleasure. Was she hoping he would destroy me? Because perhaps, that might destroy an interest in Puma that disturbed her, or shamed her?

Nobody has ever accused me of having an undernourished ego.

On the short dry grass in the walled yard we faced each other, Mike and I. If we got in, if he could get a grip on me, it would be curtains. Because he knew about leverage and anatomical vulnerability, about balance and position and strategy. If he got close, would Miss Quintana cheer?

He moved in, arms hanging in a slight arc, moving his big body with grace and economy, moving with the slowness that preceded the lunge.

I started with a sucker punch, a right hand lead. It missed the chin but caught him below the eye and the cheek reddened. I caught his nose with a straight left hand and back-pedaled hastily.

He smiled grimly, proving he wasn't hurt. He moved implacably toward me and I watched carefully, waiting for the rush.

He out-foxed me. Quicker than the eye could see, he lashed out with a sweeping left hand toward my face. It was a slap, not a punch, his hand open and his weight behind it. I went stumbling into the concrete block wall.

And he moved in.

His hand encircled my right wrist and just the pressure of it sent pain dancing along my forearm. Was that wrestling? He had said he would wrestle straight unless I pulled something raw.

He hadn't put it into writing; I had been suckered. I fought to break my wrist clear, working my weight against the thumb, but this was no ordinary thumb, and he started to twist my arm up behind me.

It was a crucial moment and I needed outside assistance. I lifted the wrist savagely, turning my body as I did, and the back of his gripping hand came in contact with the rough concrete of the wall, and I threw my body into him. He released my hand.

He grunted and stepped back, glaring at me. Blood seeped through the gashes on the back of his hairy hand, and he shook the hand absently, never taking his eyes from my face.

I fe`nted a left and caught him with a right hand in the throat. I moved around him like a lightweight, tapping him with the left hand. He smiled, to show his scorn.

Maybe in the belly? He was no kid. I moved out, in, and hit him with a real cutie, a hook off a step to the right. I hit him smack in his aging belly.

And bruised the hand. He was no kid, but his belly was. I retreated, moving far from the wall. He turned, and I turned to face him and over his shoulder I could see Miss Quintana on the redwood bench. I thought there was a look of doubt in her brown eyes.

There was no doubt in Mike's eyes. He pretended to rush, and then didn't. He stopped, and suckered me again.

This time it was a swinging right hand on the end of that long and muscular arm and rocks rattled in my thick head and nausea welled in my stomach and I forgot caution for the moment.

I moved in, bringing a right hand up from the grass. It missed the button, but caught his Adam's-apple, and he went back, gagging, fighting for breath. It can often be a near-lethal blow and as he went to one knee, I banked on that.

I came in, swinging the big right hand again like an amateur.

He ducked, and charged, throwing his shoulder into my belly and half-carried, half-shoved me back toward that concrete wall.

The speed we were moving, I had to avoid that. Even knowing the risk I'd be taking by dropping to the ground, I chanced it, and his big body fell on mine and I thought, *now he will still your wonder, Miss Quintana. . . .*

But the fiber of a man is tested by his fight in a lost cause and I must admit modestly I gave no thought to quitting.

I arched my back as I aimed a chop at his face. His head drew back to avoid it, which arched his body, and I squirmed free under the loss of contact at the fulcrum point.

I squirmed free and rolled along the grass and reached my feet before he could get to me. And now, for some reason, this was more than a test to me.

Animosity entered the picture. I hated Mike Petalious. He had never been on my Hit Parade, but I had always half-admired him, and this sudden hate is hard to explain now. Perhaps it was Miss Quintana sitting there on the bench, waiting to see me slaughtered. Or perhaps it was simply my unreasonable Italian blood boiling under competition.

I came in carelessly but confidently and I tagged him

with three lefts, a jab, a straight left and a hook, the
first two to the face, the hook to his reddened neck
where that sore Adam's-apple nestled.

I could guess by his rasping breath that his throat
was bothering him and I took the chance that it would
affect his wind. I retreated.

His hands had been up to protect his face; they lowered to wrestling position as he came after me. He was
in pain, that much was clear. He was having difficulty
getting air down his inflamed and swollen throat.

I circled, forcing him to circle. I shot a stiff left out,
not aiming for the jaw but aiming for the sore Adam's-
apple. He winced as it connected and his step faltered.
I continued to circle, and could see by the paleness on
his face that this constant circling wasn't anything he
enjoyed.

I wasn't here to make him happy. I put a fine right
hand to his nose and saw the blood start. I jabbed him
off balance and threw the big Sunday punch.

It was a bull's-eye and I can say quite modestly that
very few professionals would have come up off the floor
after that one. But Mike started to.

His legs were rubber and he would rise a completely
defenseless man, but he got to all fours and would have
made it the rest of the way from there.

I waited. Not out of any sense of decency. In this kind
of fight, I'll hit a man when he's up, down, going down
or coming up. I waited only until his chin would come
into view because one more light tap would do it.

Painfully, now, his arms pushed him higher and his
head started to raise and I got the right hand ready for
the finisher.

And from the redwood bench, Miss Quintana said,
"That will be enough. You've proved your point, you—
you *savage!*"

I turned to see her standing. And in her hand was my
gun and the business end of it was pointed right at my
stomach.

"Savage—" I said. "Whose idea was this? Not mine."

Mike, still on all fours, turned to look at her, and then
he went down again and rolled over onto his back, his
mouth open, his tortured throat sucking for air.

"You're a monster," Miss Quintana said. "Your eyes

were the eyes of an insane man. Put on your clothes
and get out of here."

I smiled at her. The gun was steady in her hand but
that didn't bother me. She wasn't used to guns. I smiled
and said, "Tell me who's the better man now?"

"It doesn't matter," she said. "On his back or on his
feet, any time and all the time, he's *my* man, and that's
what's important. Now, get out of here."

"Gladly," I answered. "Why should I stay if you're a
one-man woman?"

"And he's a one-woman man," she said. "Not a stink-
ing tomcat, like some I've heard of."

I went over to put on my socks. Mike was still on the
grass, trying to get air. I said, "If you've heard of me
you must have asked about me. Do you want to tell me
why you asked about me?"

"Get dressed," she said, "and shut up."

I put on my shoes and went over to get the harness
to strap on. I finished that and looked at the gun in her
hand. "It fits in the holster here," I explained. "May I
have it now?"

She stared at it and at me. She said softly, "You have
no idea how close I came to using it."

"I wasn't worried," I said. "You had the safety on.
Good luck, Miss Quintana."

She stared at me and there was doubt in her face, and
I thought I could see the first glimmer of the old wonder. I winked at her.

She said in a near whisper, "He's a good man. He's
kind and dependable and gentle and strong."

"I'm gentle," I told her, "and stronger. But I'll grant
you I'm not good or kind or dependable." I took a
breath. "You made the right choice."

"Choice . . . ?" she said. "There never was any question of choice."

"Yes there was," I told her gently and left her staring.

Einar Hansen's place was closed; I drove on to Dune
Street. The ancient Chev was on the lot and I hoped she
wasn't at the beach. It was a cool day but there was no
telling with these beach hounds.

She came to the door in a Hoover apron, her hair wet
and her hands stained with henna.

"Now it can be told," I said. "You had me fooled."

"I'm trying something new. What happened to your face? It's red."

"I was wrestling with my little nephew. How·about a beer?"

"Come in. It's in the refrigerator. I'll be through in a minute."

I went into the kitchen while she went back to the bathroom. I called, "Do you want a beer, too?"

"I'll get it myself when I'm through here. What's new? Did you see those men again?"

"Yup," I said. I took out a can of beer and rummaged through the drawers until I found an opener. I took the can out to the living room.

"Go on," she called. "You saw them again and what—?"

"And they told me you used to go with Einar Hansen. Then you wearied of him. But last night he spent a couple of hours here and they wondered why."

She came to the bathroom doorway, a towel around her head. She stared at me. "Do you think they'll come back here to bother me?"

"It's possible. You could move into my place until this blows over. We wouldn't have to do anything wrong unless you insisted on it."

She took a deep breath. "You simply haven't one shred of finesse, have you?"

I said thoughtfully, "You could be right. I'll bet that's what the skinny guy at the Palladium had, finesse. I'll bet that was his secret."

"You're crazy," she said. "You're absolutely, positively crazy."

"I'm disenchanted," I answered. "I'm tired and my mind wanders. Fix your hair and we'll talk sensibly."

Her voice was quieter. "What's wrong, Joe?"

"Me, you, all the people in this mess. They're all wrong. I go around and around and get nowhere. I get bruised and bloody, insulted and dismissed, looked down on and lectured."

"For money," she pointed out. "Duncan Guest was no friend of yours. You work for money and I'm sure you charge extra for all those indignities you mentioned."

"I charge extra, but it doesn't quite pay for them. Finish your hair."

She came out in a few minutes, her hair bound by a towel. She went to the kitchen and opened a can of beer and brought it out to the living room.

She sat in a chair on the other side of the room and sipped the beer. She said, "They must have been watching this place last night. How else would they know about Einar?"

"They must have been watching," I agreed. "And now they're looking for Einar and they can't find him. Do you know where he is?"

She shook her head.

"What did he want with you, last night?"

She made a face.

"Don't be coy," I said. "He wanted something besides that. He wanted information, didn't he?"

She hesitated, and nodded. "He wanted to be sure I had seen the woman in the mink stole. He wanted to know how I could be sure it was cerulean, when there was no light on the runway out there."

"That was a point that bothered me, too. How did you answer it?"

"Duncan's lights were on. His door was open and all that light was coming out on the runway."

"Just a second," I said. "His lights weren't on and the door wasn't open when I found his body."

"I know it. I turned out the light and closed the door."

"And didn't see his body in the bathroom?"

"That's right. About half an hour after the girl left, I saw the light was still on and the door open. I went to the door, called to him, and he didn't answer. I assumed he was gone. So I turned out the light and closed the door."

"And why didn't you tell the police that?"

"Would you, if you were a girl and you lived here alone and you used to go out with Duncan Guest?"

"I'm not sure," I said honestly. "Knowing the police and the newspapers in this town, I guess I wouldn't."

She fiddled with the towel on her head. "He must suspect something, don't you think? And maybe is trying to make some money out of it?"

"He doesn't seem like a blackmailer," I said.

"He knows all the wrestlers and all about them. The stories he's told me—"

"You couldn't tell whom he suspected by his line of questioning?"

She shook her head gravely. "He's clever. And as for his being a blackmailer, I think, for enough money, he would be anything."

I didn't answer. It was very quiet for a few moments. She said, "I'm frightened. I wasn't before, but I am now."

"I don't blame you," I said. "Look, if you want to play it the maidenly way, I can stay here for a few days and you can use my apartment. It might be wise."

"I wouldn't be afraid to stay with you," she answered. "I think you're probably a real gentleman, underneath it all."

"Those are the worst kind, gentlemen," I told her. "And you should know it. The Duncan Guest kind. The Gregory Harvest kind."

"Who's Gregory Harvest?"

"Duncan's lawyer. Didn't you ever meet him?"

She shook her head.

"He was right next door this noon, picking up Guest's clothes."

"I wasn't here this noon."

"Why don't we go look at the water?" I asked. "I like to look at it on these gray, gloomy days."

"All right. I guess a towel around my head won't bother anyone on the beach."

We went out to the beach and we sat where Deborah and I had sat. I wanted to get her away from that apartment, to fix her mind on something besides the apartment next door and the two hoodlums and the suddenly inquisitive Einar Hansen. She lived alone and loved it but she wasn't really self-sufficient.

We talked about dances and dancing, the Palladium and the Arragon, Benny Goodman and Lawrence Welk and about a few recent movies. She seemed to need to talk, as though it was some kind of catharsis after her original miffed semisilence.

"Irish," I said, "we started out with the lovely, nasty kind of relationship we both cherish and now we're getting to be friends. It's kind of revolting."

"I'm naturally friendly," she said, "and so are you. Couldn't we have dinner together? Dutch."

"Not Dutch," I said. "I never go Dutch."

"Even with Deborah Huntington? Or does she pay?"

I looked at her levelly. "Stop that."

"I hate her," she said, "but I'll stop."

In many ways, that afternoon and evening were a replica of my afternoon and evening with Deborah, but there were a few minor differences and one essential one.

We went to the Fox and Hounds for dinner and I paid the bill, two minor differences. We went to a movie after that, another minor change.

And then, when I took her home, she stood on the runway in front of her door and said, "I'm scared. I'm scared green. Couldn't I go home with you?"

"Of course," I told her, some quiver in my voice.

"I'll get a few things," she said.

Well, what would you think?

You're wrong.

She came to my place and I went through the elaborate and (I was sure) unnecessary routine of fixing her bed on the studio couch and taking the other half of it into my dinette for me, the pressure in me mounting all the while, the sense of imminent ecstasy bursting in me.

I mean, through it all, she was so natural and *friendly*. Even though it was plain to my practiced eye that she was quivering in anticipation of ecstasy herself.

And we bedded down in our separate compartments, both, I was sure, laughing inwardly at the fraudulence of it all.

And I lay awake a long time, waiting. She was my guest; I was the host. Sexual deportment decreed she must make the first move.

She never did. We slept through until morning, and I never laid a hand on her. That was the essential difference.

In the morning, I smelled coffee and wakened to see her in my little kitchen. Outside, it was gray, and I called, "What time is it? It looks early."

"It's almost seven o'clock, lazy-bones. Rise and shine."

"Seven o'clock. What's your hurry?"

She turned to smile at me.

And then I remembered, and I asked, "Don't you work nights?"

"Not Monday nights. I work at Streeter's."

Streeter's was a nightclub, a barn of a place, with comics and dancing girls, jugglers and crooners.

"What do you do there?" I asked.

"I dance in the chorus," she said. "Get up; the morning's half gone."

There is Joe Puma for you, all night in the same apartment with a chorus girl and didn't lay a hand on her. That should silence my occasional critics.

I was in the bathroom when there was a knock at the door. Sheila called, "I'll go. I'm dressed."

The bathroom door was closed, but it isn't thick. Through it, I recognized the voice of Detective Dolan, Sergeant Macrae's side-kick.

"I've been looking for you," he said, "since three this morning. I never thought of looking here. Where's Puma?"

"He'll be right out," she said. "What's the trouble, officer?"

"Maybe I'd better come in," he said. "I don't like to talk for the neighbors' benefit."

"Of course," she said.

I heard the door close, and I tied up my robe and went out. Dolan looked at me and then at Sheila and shook his head. "Cozy, aren't you?"

"She was frightened," I said. "Those hoodlums watched her apartment for two hours Sunday night and not a cop molested them. She was promised police protection."

Dolan said cynically, "She can't expect the Department to give her the same service you do, Puma. Most of the boys are married."

"Easy, now," I warned him. "Things are not always as they seem to people with vulgar minds."

He sniffed. He said, "I suppose you two figure you'll be each other's alibi, huh?"

"Alibi—" I stared at him, "Alibi for what?"

He held out a hand, palm up, in front of Sheila. A jet pendant earring lay there. "Recognize it?"

She nodded. "It's mine. Where's the other one?"

"Don't you know?"

She shook her head timidly. "I lost a pair like that some months ago. I'm sure it's mine."

A silence, and I asked, "What's the story, Officer? Where did you find the earring?"

"In Einar Hansen's closed, dead hand," he answered. "He was killed last night, murdered."

TEN

"DON'T BE a damned fool," Macrae said. "Of course I'm going to hold her. That was a stupid question."

We were back in the same airless room in the Venice Station, but it wasn't hot today. The morning was still cold and gray.

I asked, "Hold her for what?"

"Suspicion of murder," he said. "She lusted for him and he jilted her, didn't he? And Hansen's got her earring, hasn't he, in his cold hand?"

"But she was with me," I said. "She was with me every minute since two o'clock yesterday afternoon."

"Huh!"

"Are you calling me a liar, Sergeant?"

"I said 'Huh!' and I'll say it again. *Huh!*"

I took a deep breath and fought my temper. I said calmly, "Maybe Guest jilted her. But why would she kill Hansen?"

"Because Hansen knew she killed Guest. Why else? Or maybe Hansen jilted her, too, huh? You'd better not jilt her, Puma."

"If you book her on suspicion of murder, Sergeant," I said steadily, "you are going to make an ass of yourself. Because I'm telling you the honest-to-God truth; she was with me every minute since yesterday afternoon. I'll bet her neighbors noticed her car on the lot all that time."

"Which proves what? Only that you drove her over to Hansen's house, so she could kill him."

"Slow down," I said. "You're getting more absurd every second."

He colored and his voice shook. "*You* slow down, Puma. You're in real hot water. Maybe you didn't know

Gregory Harvest complained about you yesterday. And maybe you didn't know he's a very good friend of the District Attorney's."

"I don't worry about Gregory Harvest, Sergeant. You should, though. He's likely to be in both these murders right up to the last curl on his pretty head."

"Huh!" he said again. "Jesus, you are reaching now, aren't you?"

I didn't answer that. I asked calmly, "May I use your phone?"

"Once," he said. "One call, that's the privilege."

I phoned my attorney, Tom Devlin. He wasn't in, but I gave my story to his partner and he promised Tom would phone me as soon as he came in.

I sat back and lighted a cigarette, and Macrae said, "I won't slap you in a cell if you promise to sit there and keep your mouth shut. You can manage that for an hour or two, can't you?"

I nodded.

I sat and watched him function, the hub of half-a-dozen spokes out in the working world now going around with questions. I saw his certainty waver as they sent in their reports. I had a nosey neighbor who had seen me come home with a woman around eleven o'clock and who would swear neither of us had left before three, when she had finished the late, late, late, late show on Channel Eleven. Sheila had a friend she had told about the lost earrings two months ago. I had a former client who had seen Sheila and me enter the theater and would testify we were there when he left.

The reports came in and then Tom Devlin, my attorney, phoned. And I told him, "I don't think I'll need you, Tom. I'll call back if I do."

Macrae said, "Maybe you won't, but she sure as hell will."

I said politely, "If I'm her alibi, she's mine."

"For Einar Hansen, maybe. There was another man killed, Guest, let us not forget."

"And she wasn't even under suspicion for that. Why now?"

"So Hansen's killed and he's trying to point a finger, what would he do, if he had a minute before he died? He'd try to show us, some way, who killed Guest, right?

So he'd take one of the earrings in his hand, right?"

"Not in a million years, unless he was an English mystery writer," I said. "If he thought he was going to die, he'd get to his phone and call a doctor. He wouldn't give the tiniest damn if Guest's murderer was ever found. Would you like something better, something more reasonable, Sergeant?"

He leaned back in his chair. "I'm waiting."

"I'll bet when Sheila Gallegan checks back, she'll remember she probably left her earrings in Duncan Guest's apartment. Guest's killer probably found them there and thought they were valuable. When he, or she, learned they weren't, the killer figured it would be a good way to throw suspicion on whoever owned them. The earring is a red herring."

"I don't think the person who killed Duncan Guest was there to rob him."

"Probably not. But so the trip shouldn't be a total loss, what's wrong with picking up anything valuable around? Guest wasn't going to use them any more."

"You're wild," he said. "I'm holding her."

"You were going to hold me, too, until the reports started to come in. Are you holding her out of resentment, Sergeant?"

He said quietly, "Apologize."

"I apologize. Will you admit, though, holding her doesn't make much sense?"

"I'll hold her for her own protection," he said. "I'll hold her here, not take her to my house, like you did." He grimaced. "That's why you took her to your place, wasn't it, for her own protection?"

"Believe it or not, that's true, Sergeant. And I'll tell you something even stranger—we didn't even hold hands, all night."

He nodded. "I believe both of those statements to the same degree. You're not that old and she's not that ugly."

I said nothing.

He said softly, "Okay, Joe, I almost believe you. Dolan told me there were two beds rumpled. You admit it's hard to believe, don't you?"

"May I see her?" I asked. "I want to find out if I should get a lawyer for her."

"You can see her. For ten minutes."

"Did you pick up Koski and his buddy yesterday?"

He nodded. "And they'll come up for assault. With a big lawyer representing them, probably, and they'll get off. They weren't armed, they claimed."

"They're out on bail now?"

He nodded.

"They could have killed Einar Hansen. They told me they'd been looking for him."

"They've been checked. And they're covered for the time. They were at Mike Petalious' house, playing cards. Mike wasn't the only player to testify for them. There was a Santa Monica Police Officer in the game, too."

"What was his name?"

"What difference does it make?"

"Sheila Gallegan has a friend in the Santa Monica Department. I wondered if, by coincidence, it could be the same man."

He smiled. "You doubt her, too, do you?"

"I doubt everybody," I said. "I'll go see her now."

She had a cell all to herself and she was sitting stiffly on the cot in there, staring at the bars opposite, her face showing no evidence of recent tears.

"Sergeant Macrae," I told her, "has no case and I think he half knows it. He claims he wants to hold you for your own protection. Do you have a lawyer, or should I have mine come down for you?"

"Lawyers cost money," she said.

"Mine won't cost you anything. I'll put him on the expense account for me."

She looked at me anxiously. "That would be dishonest."

I nodded and smiled. "There are times, honey, when the only thing to do is be dishonest."

"All right," she said quietly.

I said, "Think back. Couldn't you have left those earrings in Duncan Guest's apartment some—day or night?"

"I've been thinking back," she answered, "and I could have. I'm almost sure I did, but maybe it's because I want to believe it so much. And then, of course, they aren't unique in any way. Hundreds just like them must be around this town."

"Weren't they expensive? The one I saw looked expensive."

"They were seventeen dollars. There are expensive earrings that look just like that to a layman. But these weren't."

"Well," I said, "they've checked some of your friends and one of them told the officer you had lost the earrings months ago. And the Sergeant knows now that you couldn't have killed Hansen. So there's really not a hell of a lot to worry about at the moment."

"At the moment. . . ? Will there be, later?"

"I don't know. If the killer thinks you know what Einar must have learned, perhaps. Have you told me everything you and Hansen talked about?"

She nodded slowly. "I'm sure I have. I'll try to think back carefully though. When will your lawyer be here?"

"I'll phone right now. Is it all right if I leave? You won't feel I'm deserting you?"

"I'll be all right," she said.

I went to the iron door, and she said, "Joe?"

I turned. "Yes?"

"I'm—sorry about last night. I—wanted to come over but I—didn't want to be pushy."

I smiled tolerantly. "Don't hate yourself. There'll be other nights, happier nights. Chin up, now."

She put her chin up and blew me a kiss.

That skinny bastard at the Palladium should see me now. Some of the cruds that drip dragged home. . . . I went to Macrae's room and phoned my attorney and then went out into the gray morning with renewed confidence.

We never had got to the breakfast she'd been preparing. I was planning my menu when I saw the Cadillac at the curb. Mike Petalious got out of it as I came along the walk.

"I've been waiting for you," he said. "Mr. Giampolo wants to see you."

"I've got to have breakfast first," I said. "Tell your boss I'll drop out there right after I eat."

"He don't like to wait," Mike said.

"That is very damned unfortunate. I don't intend to go to his house hungry. Now, run along, little messenger, and tell him that."

He looked me up and down, smiling slightly. "You

were lucky last time, Puma. But we'll meet again, under my terms."

"Live well until we do," I told him. "Give my regards to the missus."

"Not that it's any of your damned business," he said, "but we're getting married Saturday."

"You can thank me for that," I told him. "I proved to her you were vulnerable and she moved in for the kill. Will all the Lindsay Hall girls be there?"

"I've got a memory," he said.

He and Adonis, a great pair of mouth fighters. Mike had had his chance and not made it; would Adonis ever go into action? Koski and his buddy scared me more. They had been brought up in a world without referees and didn't need an audience.

The *Times* I read with my breakfast was too early to have the story of Sheila being found in my apartment. She was listed as missing in this edition. The old picture of her crying in front of her apartment was run again and a picture of Einar Hansen that must have been taken when he graduated from junior high school. He looked about twelve, a beardless, vapid youngster.

He had been stabbed to death, stabbed in the throat.

That didn't look like a hoodlum operation. Women killers tend to stick with stabbing. Very few women are familiar with firearms but all of them are familiar with knives and ice picks. And even a few remember that old chasity-saver, the hat-pin.

There was no mention of Joe Puma in this account; I wondered if Officer Dolan had been thoughtless enough to tell the reporters where Sheila Gallegan had finally been found. If he had, it would make a later edition. My reputation wouldn't be changed much by the revelation but I hated to think Sheila would suffer heedlessly. It had all been perfectly innocent, as related.

The sun was starting to break through as I headed for Arnold Giampolo's. I was probably heading for another lecture and it seemed unfair to me that I should get them constantly from *both* sides of the law. But he was rich and influential and someday he might need a private investigator.

He wasn't in his back yard today. He was in his living room, listening to some opera or other on a built-in hi-fi. The sound seemed to come from the lofted ceiling, but the controls were built into a stand at the side of his overstuffed chair.

"Some deal," I commented.

"Plays all my records," he said, "automatically. Seven thousand of them, on both sides. Cost me a fortu e." He nodded toward a davenport. "Sit down, Mr. Puma."

I sat down and smiled at him.

He didn't smile back at me. "Who told you about me?"

"I don't care to answer that, Mr. Giampolo."

"Gregory Harvest did, didn't he?"

I said nothing.

"Ambitious man," he said musingly. "Friend of yours?"

"No."

He looked at me thoughtfully. "You gave Koski and Kranyk to the police, but you didn't give them my name. Why not?"

"Well, first of all, I had reason to hate that pair. You haven't given me any reason to hate you." I paused. "Yet. And second, you're rich and they're not. Most of my business comes from rich people."

He frowned. "I can never tell when you're being serious. You leave an impression of *never* being serious."

"I try not to be," I explained, "in order to retain my sanity. In a world as absurd as the one we inhabit, Mr. Giampolo, sanity is not always a virtue."

He half-smiled. He said nothing.

"Look at you," I went on. "A paisan. Money enough to buy all the wine and pizzas a wop could ever eat and all the babes he could ever lay. Are you happy, as you should be? No. You take this world too seriously."

"Not this world," he said. "The next one. My doctor tells me I have about eighteen months."

Nobody said anything for seconds.

Finally I said, "I'm very sorry, Mr. Giampolo."

He nodded, saying nothing.

I asked, "Was that all you wanted to see me about, to ask about Greg Harvest?"

"Mostly. And to tell you that Harvest is a man to watch. I think he's blackmailing Deborah Huntington. Is she your client?"

I hesitated and nodded.

He said, "Miss Huntington I only know casually and by reputation, but if she could sacrifice you to get rid of Harvest, I'm sure she has the moral invulnerability to do it without flinching. So you be very wary of that pair. Now, Miss Gallegan is something else. I'm sure she knows more than she's revealed to either you or the police, but I'm not sure why she's been secretive. However, I would not consider her as dangerous as either Miss Huntington or Mr. Harvest. Have I told you anything you don't know?"

"Yes. And why?"

He frowned again. "Why. . . ? Why what?"

"Why are you anxious to help me?"

"For two reasons," he said. "First, you're a paisan. You—rather remind me of myself at your age. And second, I'd like to keep wrestling the way it is, a harmless and lucrative farce. I have a number of friends in the field and I would like to think they would continue to prosper after I am gone."

"You feel that wrestling, then, had nothing to do with the death of Duncan Guest or Einar Hansen?"

"I do. Though I have nothing but my intuition and my judgment to substantiate that feeling." He paused. "And that doesn't mean of course that a wrestler, *as an individual,* might not have killed them both."

"I understand. And using your intuition and your judgment, who would be your choice as the killer?"

He smiled weakly. "Gregory Harvest. But that might be a purely emotional judgment."

"And the girl in the white sheath dress?"

"I have no idea. Frankly, when I first read about her, I thought of Miss Quintana. I saw her in a white sheath dress one time and it was a sight I'll never forget. But this girl Miss Gallegan saw appears to have been smaller and I'm sure Miss Quintana had no reason to kill Duncan Guest."

"She hated him."

"Dozens of people did. Miss Quintana is such a well adjusted woman, I can't think of anything but a threat to Mike that would disturb her calm."

"Maybe Duncan Guest was a threat to Mike. Miss Quintana slapped my face simply because I gave the police Mike's name."

"I'm sure that wasn't the only reason. She probably feels exceptionally uncomfortable around you."

"Why should she?"

"Because you could very easily be the first man she's met since tying up with Mike who makes her think of some man besides Mike. As a matter of fact, after your first visit, Mike told me you had impressed her. He was a little worried for the first time since I've known him."

I shook my head sadly. "And I had to get on the wrong side of her. You know, at first a person thinks of her as a big woman. But after seeing her a few times, she doesn't look big at all. And all other women look like misshapen midgets."

He didn't seem to be listening, staring the length of his big living room.

I stood up. "Thanks for your interest, Mr. Giampolo."

He looked at me and nodded. "Mr. Harvest will undoubtedly represent Koski and Kranyk in court. Don't let that indicate to you that I sent him because he's a friend of mine. He isn't."

I smiled. "Not a friend, only a partner. Has Devine got a piece of the top, too?"

He shook his head. "And Mr. Harvest won't have his long. I think Mike Petalious would make an efficient heir, don't you?"

"It would be a nice gesture for his loyalty," I said. "And then his wife would be able to mix with her old friends again."

"But she's not his wife."

"They're being married Saturday."

"Strange he didn't tell me." Giampolo smiled. "Maybe you're responsible for the wedding. Maybe you did Miss Quintana a favor, Joe."

"You overrate me," I said. "Mr. Giampolo, have you been all over for your medical opinions? Have you been to Rochester?"

"I've been to Rochester," he said. "As for going around the world for medical opinions, I didn't have to. I sent for them and they came and the eighteen months is an outside figure."

"I'm sorry," I said again.

"Good day, Mr. Puma. It's time for my nap."

I went to the office. There was no mail of importance. I called my phone-answering service and was informed a Miss Huntington had phoned at ten this morning and would except me to return the call.

I didn't do it right away. I typed up all the reports of my travels since last I had sat here and read those along with the previous reports. There were a number of lies apparent in the conflicting testimony but none of it was consistent enough to point a finger.

I was pulling the carbon copies to mail to Macrae when my phone rang and it was Deborah.

"I left a message for you to call me," she said stiffly. "Where have you been?"

"I just this second walked into the office, Deb. I've been busy."

"I'll bet. I see you and Miss Gallegan are getting better acquainted."

"Where did you see that?"

"In the afternoon paper. It didn't make the morning papers."

"I know," I said. "I'm sorry it had to make any paper. Nothing happened, Deb. Not that you'd care if it had."

"You're right; it's none of my business. But was it necessary to attack Creg Harvest?"

"I didn't attack him and if he told you I did, he's a liar. He wanted to fight me and I let him off easy. We just shook hands."

A pause. "I should have trusted my first feeling about you. I would like to cancel our contract. I don't feel that you're the proper man to investigate this murder."

"You could be right," I said. "I'll bill you for the work already performed. I'll pick up the tab on that evening at The Elms. For auld lang syne."

"Suit yourself," she said. "Good-bye, Joe. Good luck."

"Thank you," I said. "Good luck to you." I replaced the receiver quickly.

The phone rang again almost immediately but I didn't answer it. I stacked the carbons for Macrae. I hadn't mentioned Giampolo in these reports and that was dishonest, but I told myself Giampolo wasn't important to this murder and if he had told me the truth he wouldn't be a threat to law and order much longer. Let him die in peace.

The phone continued to ring. It was still ringing when I went out.

ELEVEN

EINAR HANSEN had lived in a beach shack not too far from the Koski-Kranyk apartment in Playa del Rey. He had lived there with his sister; she was not home. She had not been home early last night, either; she had been visiting an aunt in Encino when her brother had been stabbed to death.

At the shack next door, a fat woman in blue jeans and sweat shirt was watering the patch of Bermuda grass in front that served for a lawn.

"She ain't home," she called to me. "You selling something?"

"No," I said. "I'm a detective." I went over there.

She squinted at me. "I know you. You were in the papers. Joseph Puma, right?"

"Right as rain, m'am."

"You know my husband, Whitey Tullgren, right?"

I had put his buddy in San Quentin for nine years, but my testimony had helped to keep Whitey free. I said, "Hell, yes, I know him. How is he doing now?"

"Great," she said. "He's a bouncer at the Red Mill. He's fishing today. Whitey thinks a lot of you, Mr. Puma."

"I'm glad to hear it," I said. "On the straight and narrow, is he? I knew he could make it."

"Could you go for a beer?" she asked.

"I certainly could," I said. "That sun finally came out, didn't it?"

She nodded. "We'll have to drink it on the porch. Whitey finds me in the house with a man, he'd cut my legs off at the knee."

"I don't blame him," I said. "Too many wolves around these days."

She laughed cynically. "Save it, Mr. Puma. I got a mirror. And a scales. I'll get the beer."

I sat on the porch in a rattan rocker and looked out at the sand and the sea and the Hyperion Sewage Disposal Plant. The wind was from the shore today and there was no discernible odor.

116

Mrs. Tullgren came out with two cans of beer and handed me one. She sat nearby in a rattan armchair. "Einar's sister is at the funeral home, arranging things. There was just the two of them; their folks is dead."

"Terrible thing," I said. "Doesn't make any kind of sense at all to me. Einar was not a violent man, was he?"

"Einar? No. Smart, though. I always had the feeling he picked up a dirty dollar now and then. That hamburger stand wasn't exactly a gold mine."

"No," I agreed. "Nothing personal, now, but he wasn't living in Beverly Hills, either."

"He owned the place next door. He supported his sister. He bought a new Chev every year and owned seven acres out in Palos Verdes. Would he get all that out of a hamburger stand?"

"It's possible."

"No, it ain't. I know what his daily take averaged."

Silence. I sipped the beer and looked at the off-shore oil derricks to the north. I said casually, "I'll bet you know more than that."

"Maybe. I sleep nights, too. And got Whitey right next to me in bed, warm and snuggy. Who wants trouble?"

"Not you," I said. "Not Whitey."

"Right!"

I didn't press her. She was dying to tell me, panting to give me all the gossip. I said, "I used to know Whitey at the Arragon. He could really dance."

"We still do, all the time. Square dancing, though. Three times a week."

"I could never see that," I said. "Ballroom dancing, yes. But those squares give me a laugh."

"Wait'll you're our age. You'll like it."

I sipped my beer and looked at the ocean.

"The cops were here," she said, "asking did we see anything next door last night. I told 'em we didn't. Whitey don't want any part of cops, with him or against him. We didn't see anything, we said."

"His sister found him, when she came home—is that the way it was?"

"Right." A pause. "If I tell you something, you tell the cops and they come back at me. That's the way it would be, ain't it?"

"No," I said. "I can keep my mouth shut. And if I collect any reward, I can send you fifty bucks if you know something that helps."

"But you're working with the cops."

"True. And for myself. You and Whitey would never be mentioned, unless it was necessary and you gave me permission."

"Forget the fifty," she said, "You done enough for Whitey already. One thing his sister told me yesterday morning and I didn't see in the paper, she told me Einar practically insisted she had to run up to the Valley to see that aunt. Funny, huh?"

"Maybe he figured it was his sister's duty. With their parents dead, maybe Einar thought they should keep up the family relationships they did have."

"Naw. Or he'd have gone along. He didn't have the stand open yesterday; he wasn't working. And the aunt didn't have no money. Money, that's what Einar loved, not relatives."

"You figure somebody was coming to see him and he wanted his sister out of the way?"

"That's what I figured and that's what happened. He had a visitor, a blond guy in a Jaguar."

"You mean the killer was a blond man driving a Jaguar?"

"I wouldn't say that, not for sure. He could have been. I didn't see nothing in the paper about him. And Whitey thought he heard another car earlier." She paused. "We were—uh—busy then. This blond guy was there around one o'clock."

"How could you see him in the dark?"

"He left his lights on. I suppose so he could see his way over there. No moon last night, you know. You want another beer?"

"I hate to be a pig," I said, "but I could use one. It's sure restful, sitting here."

"Ain't it?" she agreed. "Nothing fancy, but Whitey and me, we love it here." She got up and went into the house.

I looked over at the house of Einar Hansen. Beyond it, in the background, was the Hyperion Sewage Disposal Plant. To the north was the Santa Monica Yacht Basin and the curving line of the shore all the way to Point Dume. For a low-rent district, the Tullgrens enjoyed an impressive view.

Einar Hansen, blackmailer. . . . I wouldn't have thought it. Had he known at the time who had killed Duncan Guest or had he figured it out later or had he simply played a hunch? All this was only surmise; I had no facts to discredit Einar Hansen.

Mrs. Tullgren handed me another can of beer and I thanked her. She said, "Nice view, ain't it?"

"Very nice. Do you own this place?"

"In fifteen years we'll own it. We bought it five years ago. Twenty-year mortgage."

"You might even have some oil. Those derricks are pretty close."

"Who needs oil? I got Whitey and Whitey's got me and we dance three times a week. You see many of them rich couples dancing three times a week?"

"I guess you're right. Whitey's happy, too?"

"Hell, yes. If we could have had a couple kids, now, we'd both be happier, but you can't have *everything*, right?"

"That blond man in the Jaguar, how old would you guess he was?"

"In his thirties. About your age. College kid type. Had one of those tan car coats on." She sipped the beer. "I couldn't be sure, but it looked like a woman waited in the car. Make sense to you?"

"It could. I know a man like that, a lawyer. But he's too sharp for me. All the bright ones are."

"That ain't the way Whitey talks about you. He says you're a real brain."

"I'm not, Mrs. Tullgren. Look, I'm going to tell this man with the Jaguar, that I saw him in this neighborhood last night. I won't mention you or Whitey, under any circumstances. Okay?"

"Fair enough," she said. "Glad to be of help."

I finished my beer and thanked her and left. I was glad to see Whitey on the right side of the law; I'd always liked him, a man who enjoyed every second, drunk or sober.

I drove over to Wilshire and headed toward the Arena. I was no longer representing a client in this business, but there was still the reward Adonis had posted. Even if there had been no reward, I was involved, now, and had no other job that needed my attention.

I was backing into a parking space a half block from

the Arena when a Continental stole it from me, sliding into it from behind.

I turned around, growling, and looked into the amused grimace of Deborah Huntington. She thumbed her nose at me.

I found another space a little further up the street. As I walked back, I saw Deborah waiting for me next to her car. I didn't smile.

"Sour-puss," she said.

"Good afternoon, Miss Huntington," I said. "Visiting your lover or your brother?"

"Curt. Is Greg my lover now?"

"You were with him last night, weren't you? He claims you were."

"Would that make him my lover? Lover connotes something beyond a casual date now and then."

"I'll take the word back. I'll call him your friend. And what were you and your friend doing at Einar Hansen's last night? And if one of you didn't kill him, why didn't you tell the police you were there?"

We both stood next to her car now and she stared at me doubtfully. "I wasn't with Greg last night. If he told you that, he lied."

"*Now* you deny it. You didn't before."

She took a deep breath. "I didn't know you were serious. I was trying to tease you." She put a hand on my arm. "Was Greg there last night? Are you sure of it?"

I nodded.

"I tried to call you back this afternoon," she said. "I was angry, and I didn't mean to say what I did. I'm still your client, Joe."

"I'll think about it."

She looked up anxiously. "What's happened to you? My God, you can't think I'm a murderer!"

"It isn't that. You're too emotionally erratic. I don't like to be a victim of your iron whim."

She smiled. "I thought you were tougher. You're not really very tough, are you?"

I didn't answer her. I started to walk toward the arena. She walked along next to me. "Will you come up to Curt's office after you see Greg? He'd be interested, I'm sure, in Greg's extracurricular activities."

"I'll be up there," I promised.

"Where have you been today?" she asked. "With Sheila Gallegan?"

"She was still in jail, the last time I saw her. Which reminds me, I'll have to phone my attorney to see if he got her released. I'll use Curt's phone for that, I guess. Harvest might be uncooperative."

"I doubt if he's there," she said. "He usually plays golf on Tuesday afternoons."

At the entrance to Greg's office, Deborah went on and I turned in. Greg's secretary looked up, frowned, and said, "Oh, yes, Mr. Puma."

"You remembered me," I said admiringly. "Is Curly in?"

"Mr. Harvest is playing golf," she said smugly. "Is there any message, Mr. Puma?"

"It's—rather personal," I answered. "Tell him I'll phone him later. Would it be all right if I used his phone to make another call?"

"You could use this phone," she said. "His office is locked."

I used her phone to call Tom Devlin and he told me Sheila Gallegan had been released two hours ago. I asked him how much of a case they had against her.

"None," he said. "Sergeant Macrae down there is talking big, but the D.A. wouldn't think of going into court on what they have. The girl a client of yours or just a friend, Joe?"

"What difference does it make?"

"None. But I took her home and it's obvious that she's poor and I wondered what she'd pay you with, if she was a client."

"You have a pornographic imagination, haven't you? She's a friend and you may send your bill to me and keep your hot little hands to yourself."

"If that's the way you want it, Joe. I'm kind of expensive, these days." He hung up.

In the chair behind her small desk, Harvest's secretary was all ears and big eyes. I said into the phone, "And another thing, Tom, Harvest's secretary is okay. Don't listen to those rotten things Greg was saying about her."

I hung up and flexed a muscle in my jaw, like Greg Harvest does.

His secretary said, "You're so funny. I'm surprised a

man with all your talent has to wear such cheap suits."

I flexed another jaw muscle, sighed, smiled at her tolerantly and went out.

The gym was deserted, smelling of liniment, canvas and sweat. In Curtis Huntington's outer office, his elderly secretary waved me through with a smile.

I went in to find Curt standing at the window, looking out at the traffic on Wilshire. Deborah sat in a pull-up chair near his desk.

He turned and said, "Deb has told me about Harvest being at Hansen's last night. Shouldn't we tell the police that?"

"Not yet," I said.

"Why not?"

I didn't want to tell him I couldn't be sure it was Greg. I said, "I've some other things to tell you about him first."

He came over to sit behind his desk; I pulled a chair closer and sat down.

I told him about my talk with Arnold Giampolo. I included the bit about Arnold's illness.

When I'd finished, he said, "An ambitious man, isn't he? Harvest, I mean."

"A real cutie," I admitted. "Didn't you know he was a silent partner of Giampolo's?"

Huntington shook his head. "Of course not. I couldn't afford to have a man of that calibre representing us." He looked at Deborah. "We'll have to reassess Mr. Gregory Harvest."

"I—never quite trusted him, remember," she said.

"I know, I know." He smiled weakly. "But you aren't the most consistent judge of character in the world, Deborah. Remember how you mistrusted Joe at the beginning?"

"I still do," she said. "It's his personal charm that keeps me on the hook." She looked at me. "Remember you were going to phone and find out about that Gallegan girl."

"To hell with her," I said casually. "I found out she hasn't got any money."

Curt laughed. Deborah didn't. Deborah blushed. Curt stopped laughing.

I smiled and said, "I'd like you, Deb, even if you were poor. You're prettier than she is."

"Keep talking," she said. "You've got a long way to go."

Curt said amiably, "Why don't we all have dinner together and stop feuding? We can find something besides murder to talk about, I'm sure."

Deborah said coolly, "Sorry, I have a date for dinner. As a matter of fact, I'd better get home right now. He's calling for me at seven."

She stood up, smiled at both of us, and left.

Curt smiled and sighed.

"Damned attractive girl," I said, "but she would drive a husband insane in less than a month."

He looked at me bleakly. "She wasn't very damned far from insane herself, two years ago. But she's getting more —adjusted every day. Deborah's an idealist, believe it or not."

"I believe it. Well, I'm going to look up Harvest. I want his story before I decide about telling the police. Is that okay with you?"

He smiled. "You'd have to ask Deborah. She's your client."

I said, "One thing I forgot to tell you about my talk with Arnold Giampolo—he plans on making Mike Petalious Mr. Big in the wrestling dodge."

"Good," Huntington said. "Mike's a straight-shooter, just the man to keep the game honestly crooked."

"Don't tell Harvest that," I suggested. "Mike's tough enough, but I wouldn't want to be responsible for making Harvest his enemy."

He nodded. "I'll say nothing. And what I told you about Deborah two years ago—that's strictly between *us*, of course."

"Of course," I said.

He went back to the window to look at the traffic as I went out. I was going by Greg's office when the impulse hit me, and I turned in.

His secretary was plucking her eyebrows. She looked at me coolly.

I said, "Forget my bad manners for a moment and my insolent attempts at humor. Just remember that I am licensed as an investigator by the State of California and am currently working directly with the Los Angeles Police Department on a double murder."

She sat erectly in her chair. "I'm listening."

"Did you have a date with the boss last night?"

Her face froze. "I happen to be married, Mr. Puma."

"You haven't answered my question."

"I'm busy. Good night."

"All right," I said. "But remember this, I happen to know Gregory Harvest visited the man who was killed last night. So far, I haven't told that to the police. Under certain conditions, I may never tell them. But if I do, they're going to ask him about it. And if he tells them who the girl with him was, they're going to give it to the newspapers. Believe me, lady, I'm not trying to be funny now."

She inhaled heavily and stared at the tweezers still in her hand. She didn't look at me. "Under *what* conditions are you going to keep it from the police?"

"If I decide he isn't the killer and that somebody might be hurt if I told on him. Privacy is what I sell, but I can only sell it within the law and for good reasons."

"I was with him last night," she said quietly.

"Honestly?"

She nodded mutely.

I asked, "What did he wear last night?"

"A sport coat and slacks and one of those short, tan car coats."

"Did he have a flashlight? There aren't any street lights down there."

She shook her head. "He kept the car lights on. He went up to the house and rang the doorbell, but nobody answered. Then he went to the garage and saw the car was gone so he knew Mr. Hansen wasn't home."

"Hansen was home," I said. "His sister had the car. She was up in the Valley. Didn't you read the papers this morning?"

"Of course. But I assumed they had two cars. Most people out here do, you know."

"How many times has Hansen been here in the office?"

"I'm not going to answer any more questions," she said. "I've said too much already." She looked at me dully. "I've got a jealous, impossible husband, Mr. Puma. And a three-year-old daughter whom I love very much."

"Okay," I said. "I can't promise to keep my mouth shut, but I hope I'll be able to. It depends on how cooperative Mr. Harvest is. You can tell him that."

"I'll be sure to," she said. "You won't say anything about this to the police before you talk with him, will you?"

"I promise you I won't." I started toward the door and then turned back. "What business did Mr. Harvest have with Hansen? Why did he go over there?"

"I don't know," she said. "It was something about wrestling, but I swear to you that's all he told me."

I went out and along the walk to my car. The traffic was bumper to bumper on Wilshire and the air was blue with smog. There was a calling card on my front seat, an engraved card, Deborah Huntington's.

I turned it over and read: *Get home early tonight. I have a key I stole last time I was there.*

TWELVE

WELL, TO HELL with her, blow-hot, blow-cold. Who did she think she was dealing with, some Iowa clodhopper? She was messing with a *Palladium* champion and she had better not hold her breath waiting for me to get home.

Desire moved through me and I inhaled heavily and tried to think of something else. I pulled out into traffic carelessly and heard the scream of braking tires from behind and the angry blasts from a number of horns.

What was she—a nympho and a klepto, too? Stealing my key . . . She had her nerve. I had half-a-dozen keys, but they had to be *earned*. Maybe she thought her money gave her privileges.

She was pretty, she was smart. She was passionate, she was rich. Don't be too indignant, Puma. Calm down. She means well.

A car went by on my left and the driver shouted something at me. A car went by on my right and a lady glared at me from behind the wheel. I kept my eyes to the front and drove to the office.

There, I added what little I had done since last sitting here and tried to align it with the rest, looking for the lead. Nothing, nothing, nothing. . . .

It was ready to snap at me, the obvious was, but it would only be the obvious from hindsight. There were so many cross-currents of interest, conflict of personalities, so many half-revealed animosities clouding the pure air of sweet reason.

Why does a killer kill? For money, lust, hate, greed, protection, frustration—the reasons were as vast and varied as the people who killed and were killed. Some kill in anger and some in sick objectivity and some in ecstasy.

Why did this killer kill?

I couldn't be sure the same killer had killed both Guest and Hansen, but it seemed like a reasonable surmise. Had Giampolo misled me? Had Guest, perhaps, also had a piece of the top? Giampolo would have reason to lie if that were true, as revelation would lead the police to investigate wrestling and Giampolo didn't want that. But if he had lied, had he also killed?

Harvest, it seemed, had decided to cross Giampolo. If Guest was the third partner, Harvest would have reason to kill him. Because when Giampolo died, Harvest would be the sole heir. Harvest didn't know Mike Petalious was already picked for that honor.

Did Miss Quintana know that Mike had been chosen as heir and that Guest might be a threat to that? Now, you are reaching, Puma; Lindsay Hall girls rarely murder for profit.

I thought of her in a white sheath-dress as Giampolo had once seen her and envied him the memory of it. I wondered if she had a pair of jet pendant earrings.

I ate dinner at the Horned Frog because I could walk over and wouldn't need to buck the early evening traffic. I ate slowly, trying to think, trying to find a path through the maze around the twin deaths. Perhaps it hadn't been the same killer, but I felt sure that it was.

It wasn't exactly the best time in the world to go back to the Hansen residence, after his sister had spent the afternoon at the mortician, but I drove over anyway.

The new Chev was parked at the side of the house. It was just starting to get dark and there was a light showing in the kitchen and I could see the shadow of a woman moving around in there.

The front doorbell didn't seem to be working; I knocked.

The woman who came to the door didn't look like a relative of Einar's. She was dark and short, with a full figure that just missed being chunky.

"My name is Joe Puma," I said. "Perhaps Einar has mentioned me to you?"

She nodded. "I know who you are. Mrs. Tullgren told me you were here this afternoon. Come in, Mr. Puma."

The house was brightly furnished and hospital-clean. She said, "I'm getting dinner. We can talk in the kitchen."

She stood next to the sink, dicing carrots. I sat in a chair near the rear door. I asked, "Do you think Einar sent you to the Valley yesterday so he could meet someone here?"

She shook her head. "He was always after me to go up and visit Aunt Helga. Why would he have to meet anybody here? If he didn't want me to see them, he could drive to their house, couldn't he?"

"Yes. Do you have any idea who could have—done this?"

She shook her head.

I said hesitantly, "I'm not the police, you know."

She turned around to look at me. "What does that mean? Anything I'd tell you, I'd tell the police. Einar had nothing to hide."

I asked, "Did a man named Gregory Harvest ever visit him here?"

"Not to my knowledge."

"Mike Petalious?"

"Big Greek with a good-looking wife?"

"Yes."

"They were here a couple days ago." She frowned. "Sunday, that was it. Sunday afternoon, Einar had a boy working the stand and he was home and this couple came over. They sat out in front and talked."

"Was it friendly talk?"

"I guess. Einar didn't seem disturbed to see them."

"Did Duncan Guest come here often?"

The woman turned around again. "Once. There was a man Einar and I didn't agree about and I told my brother I wouldn't have that man in the house. Scum, that's what he was."

"Einar thought a lot of him, didn't he?"

"I guess he did. He isn't usually that wrong about people, but he admired this Duncan Guest. Thought he was awful smart." She looked at me bleakly. "Do you think it was the same person that—that done both things?"

"It's a strong possibility. Miss Hansen, isn't there anything you can think of that might help me?"

"Nothing," she said. "Absolutely nothing, or I would have given it to the police."

I thanked her and left. She didn't seem to be mourning her brother too much; her voice had been matter of fact and well controlled. Perhaps the full realization hadn't come home to her yet. Though it must have if she had been making arrangements for the funeral this afternoon.

The water was barely visible now, and in the hills to the east, north and south the lights were going on. There were lights in the home of Whitey Tullgren and the sound of a television program.

It was suddenly cool after the heat of the day and a chill moved across my shoulders as I climbed into the Plymouth. I had nowhere to go, no lead to follow or suspect to interrogate. I was blind and somewhere a killer was laughing.

I stopped at the Venice Station. Macrae and his sidekick weren't there, but a detective who was familiar with the case talked with me in the airless room.

They had the same theory I had: the same killer had killed both men. They were nowhere, as I was. I thought of telling them what I had learned about Harvest and had not put into my report. But I thought of his secretary's three-year-old daughter and kept my mouth shut.

"What about the earring?" I asked him. "What's Macrae's theory on that?"

"The same as before, he figures it was Hansen's way of naming his killer."

"Do you?"

The detective smiled. "I wouldn't have any theories in conflict with Sergeant Macrae's right now. He's like a man with a perpetual toothache."

"Wouldn't it be more logical to think Hansen pulled it off the ear of the woman who stabbed him?"

"Maybe. That would make it Miss Gallegan, wouldn't it?"

"Not necessarily. It was a production earring; there could be thousands of them around."

"Miss Gallegan must have known that. But she claims it was hers."

I went out and it was now dark. From the direction of Santa Monica, searchlights stabbed the sky; a new supermarket was opening. The Plymouth started with a shudder and moved along Main Street with a clatter of tappets.

Nowhere, nothing, nowhere, nothing. . . . I thought of Einar Hansen's funeral coming up and of Duncan Guest's funeral, now history. Some near-revelation flickered dimly in me and died. Funeral, funeral, funeral . . . What had it tried to trigger?

I had an urge to drive over to Sheila Gallegan's, but dismissed it. I didn't want to see her tonight. I didn't want to see Deborah either and I hoped that message she'd written on her card had been a gag. Two people had died and it seemed likely their deaths would not be avenged. People die every second, I tried to tell myself.

Funeral, funeral, funeral . . . Was some truth awaiting me at Einar Hansen's funeral?

The police might have knowledge they weren't revealing to me. They had the men and the equipment, but they also had a lot of crimes to solve and too much area to patrol.

Nobody was waiting for me at my apartment. I took a hot shower, pared my toe nails, shaved, put on a pair of cotton pants and a T-shirt and sat down in front of the television set with a can of tomato juice.

Peace was starting to settle into my bones when I heard the turn of a key in my door. I put on a smile to greet her with. After all, she was rich. And had rich friends.

She came in, a quart of Jack Daniel's Tennessee Whiskey in one hand and a bottle of ginger ale in the other.

"Putting Jack Daniel's into ginger ale," I told her, "is a sacrilege I shouldn't permit under my roof."

"I don't like water," she said. "Sweet things, that's what I like Sweet, soft things."

"So do I, but not to drink. How was your dinner engagement?"

"I didn't have one. I was annoyed with you. Why do you always have to talk about rich girls, rich people, wealth It's an obsession with you."

"Isn't it with you? Don't you feel superior to most of the people you meet?"

"No," she said.

My phone rang and it was Greg Harvest. He asked, "Can I see you in about an hour? I have to talk with you."

"I don't want to see anybody," I told him. "Talk."

"Joe, don't be difficult. What happened was all very innocent and I don't want Mrs. Schroeder to get into trouble."

"Is that your secretary, Mrs. Schroeder?"

"Yes. I wouldn't mind going to the police right now and telling them about my visit to Hansen's. But I'd have to implicate her."

I said nothing.

"Can't you see that, Joe?"

"Yes. Don't worry, I promised her I wouldn't go to the police until you and I talked. Tomorrow morning at your office be all right for that? Say about ten o'clock?"

"Why can't I come over tonight?"

"Because I'm sick. My stomach is still sore from those hoodlums' kicks and it's starting to act up. The doctor is coming in a few minutes and then I'm going to bed."

"Oh. I'm sorry, Joe. Will you be all right in the morning?"

"I'm sure I will. Your office, ten o'clock?"

"Right. And thanks, Joe, for your—discretion."

"That's what I sell," I told him. "Keep it in mind."

The new Greg Harvest, the humble halfback. I hung up and turned to find Deborah staring at me.

"That was Greg Harvest," she said. "I recognized his secretary's name."

"How shrewd of you."

"What was that about going to the police? Who is the woman you promised? What's Greg trying to pull now?"

"Deb," I said patiently, "I'm a *private* investigator."

"And I'm your client and I have a right to know what's going on. You're making some kind of deal with Greg, aren't you? I'm your client, Joseph Puma."

"At the moment. Will you be tomorrow? Were you this afternoon? You're my client but not my wife."

She glared at me. "If you don't tell me exactly what all that was about, I'm leaving right now."

"Okay," I said. "Don't forget your whiskey."

"And I'm going to report you, too, to whoever issues your license.

"The Attorney General of the State of California," I
told her, "and tell him *everything*."

She stood rigidly, hate burning in her eyes. "You
damned, arrogant dago."

"You're upset," I said. "Relax. Grow up."

"I'm leaving," she said. "It's your last chance."

I smiled at her. "You sound like a bus. Don't threaten
me, Deborah. Take your whiskey and fire me for the second time today and leave with dignity, if you want to
leave. But don't storm and rant; it's been a depressing
day."

She glared for a few more seconds and then left without
another word, taking her whiskey with her. I sat in front
of the television set with the tomato juice and tried to
relax again.

Why had I handled her the way I had? Why hadn't I
smoothed her over and explained about Greg some way
and saved both her and the Jack Daniels for myself.

She was attractive, intelligent, worthwhile. In her rational periods she was fun, witty and delightfully malicious. I had courted a number of girls with a lot less; why
hadn't I saved her for tonight?

There was nothing good on television, as usual, and I
was now too disturbed emotionally to enjoy my own
company. I turned off the set and picked up a book and
it bored me. All the other books in sight I had read at some
time.

I got a big piece of paper and put down all the charac-
ters in this muddled murder and tried to connect them
with lines of meaning, tried to find in the web of inter-
connecting lines, some road to revelation. Again, some
thing flickered in my mind and I thought of a funeral,
but it wouldn't come into full reason.

I was feeling very frustrated when my doorbell rang.

I was sure it was Deborah and I was glad, because I
was not good company for myself tonight.

Sheila Gallegan stood there, a small overnight bag in
one hand. She looked at me timidly. "I—was frightened.
I thought one more night wouldn't put you out too much,
would it?"

"Not at all," I said, "if you'll help me with the beds."

She sighed and smiled. "Let's not go through that ritual
again. One bed's all right with me if it is with you."

I assured her it would be a pleasure.

THIRTEEN

GREG HARVEST's right hand was in a partial cast, across the knuckles.

I said, "My God, I didn't do that, did I?"

He nodded. "Sit down, Joe."

I sat down. We were in his office and his secretary had greeted me cordially, for a change, and so had Greg, for a change. I looked at his hand and couldn't look into his eyes.

"You're embarrassed," he said. "That's a switch."

"I'm a pugnacious ass," I said, "a vulgar wop." I met his gaze. "Not that you haven't a few faults, yourself."

He leaned back in his chair and looked at me thoughtfully. "Maybe. I went over to see Hansen Monday night because I thought he might know something about the murder. I didn't see his car there and nobody answered the door, so I assumed he was out. I wasn't there for more than a few minutes."

"A few minutes is all it would take to kill a man."

"That's true enough. Do you think I killed him, Joe?"

"I don't think about it either way. Is there more you wanted to tell me?"

He fiddled with a gold football on his desk. It was meant to go on a watch chain but he didn't wear a watch chain. He looked like he was coming to an important decision.

When he met my gaze again, he said, "I guess I'm through with the Huntingtons, finished. Do I have you to thank for that?"

I shook my head. "I didn't frame you. Every man makes his own mistakes, Greg."

"Yes. And I suppose mine was loving Deborah too much. She's a sick woman, Joe."

I said nothing.

He said, "That's why I went over to see Einar Hansen. I felt that he knew who the murderer was and I wanted to protect her any way I could."

"Her . . .?"

132

"Deborah Huntington. Who else?"

"You think she killed Guest?"

"I repeat, who else?"

"You're forgetting," I said, "that she's alibied for the time. By servants and by neighbors. By a neighbor with a first class reputation. The police have checked her very thoroughly, Greg."

"The police can never check as thoroughly as they should. There aren't enough police in this town and there are too many murders. Joe, I know her psychiatrist and he trusts me. I'm going to phone him and explain to him the importance of his telling you about Deborah Huntington."

I sat quietly, despising him. He had been thrown out by the Huntingtons and now he was trying to get back at them. I shook my head and smiled pityingly at him.

"What in hell does that mean? She got you on the hook, now?"

I shook my head again. "You hate her, now. You want to get back at her through me. That's adolescent. Grow up, Greg. Forget the glory of the past and be adult."

Irritation moved across his handsome face. "You're not getting me. I have grown up. This isn't resentment. All along, I've been trying to protect her." He took a breath. "Legally, if possible. But if that wasn't possible, any damned way I could. I tell you, I loved her."

"And still do," I said. "And if you can't have her, you intend to destroy her. Jesus, man, she hired me to find the killer."

"No. She hired you to check the trail to the killer so she could learn if there was any concealment she overlooked. She trusted her body to gain your loyalty. She probably figures any private investigator can be bought, one way or another."

His phone rang, and he picked it up irritatedly and said, "I told you I didn't want to be interrupted." A pause and then, "Oh, I'm sorry, Ruth. Put him on."

Another pause and he said, "Yes." A pause. "I'm busy now." A pause while he frowned nervously. "All right. I'll be there in an hour."

He replaced the phone and stared quietly at me.

"Deborah?" I asked.

"No. A man named Kranyk."

"Who has a friend named Koski," I added. "And the

pair of them work for a man named Giampolo and he
is worried about an ambitious young athlete named
Gregory Harvest and you are due for some lumps."

He continued to stare at me. He licked his lips. "How
much, Joe?"

"How much what?"

"How much do you want to go along?"

I looked at his hand in the narrow cast. "Nothing. I
owe you a few hours, I guess."

He lifted the damaged hand. "Because of this."

"Partly." I held my stomach. "And because of this. I
owe them something, too, but being adult, I can't strike
back without reason."

"You certainly can rationalize, can't you? I give you
a killer and you don't want to go after her, so you say
I'm resentful. I give you a chance for violence and you
consider it a license to dispense your particular kind of
justice."

I smiled at him. "I'm a temporary ally, Greg. Even
Churchill didn't talk that way about the Russians during
the war."

"Are you armed?"

I nodded. "But I doubt if they'll be. They're out on
bail, now."

His voice was tight and nervous. "How did you learn
Giampolo disliked me?"

"He told me. He's dying; did you know that?"

Harvest nodded.

"Did you figure to inherit the throne?"

He didn't answer me. He said, "We'll take my car
over to Playa del Rey. All right?"

"Why didn't they come here?" I asked, "if they only
wanted to talk with you?"

He smiled at me. He looked nervous but determined.
He didn't answer my question and there was really no
reason to.

On the way over, he told me how he'd met Deborah.
He'd met her in a bar and she'd been in the bar alone.
And looking for a man. Greg thought, but maybe it was
something he wanted to think now. She had her faults,
but he was trying to debase her even further in his memory.

"And how did you meet Giampolo?" I asked him.

"Through Duncan Guest. And I met Guest through

Luscious Louie and Louie through Deborah. She knows a lot of wrestlers."

"Guest did know Giampolo, then. Maybe that's why he died, Greg."

Harvest said evenly, "He died because he jilted Deborah. And you'll find that out, eventually."

We rode the rest of the way in silence, a silence that seemed to grow more tense as we came closer to the Playa del Rey apartment of Koski-Kranyk. It didn't seem logical to me that Harvest would go there at all if he thought they planned to harm him. But perhaps he had to go, committed as he was. And if he hadn't feared them, he wouldn't have asked me to go along.

And then from nowhere a thought came to me and I voiced it. I said, "You didn't play golf yesterday, not with that hand."

"I was up in San Francisco," he said.

"On business?"

"Yes. Legal business, legitimate business."

"Why did your secretary say you were playing golf?"

"Maybe she thought I was. What difference does it make, Joe?"

I didn't answer. Phony, phony Gregory Harvest with his new humility, his story on Deborah, his properly timed phone call. I remembered that his secretary hadn't been in his outer office when we left. Nobody had seen us leave together.

Of course, my car was still there and maybe I was seeing ghosts.

But when we parked in front and he turned his back to me to climb out of the Jag, I reached in quickly, took my .38 from its shoulder holster and put it in my jacket pocket.

What had he done in San Francisco, seen some boss higher than Giampolo?

"What are you waiting for, Joe?" he asked me.

I looked up at him, standing above me on the curb. "I'm looking for the light," I said.

He frowned. "Is something wrong? You sound punchy."

"I'm a little nervous," I said. "That's a rough pair in there."

He smiled. "All right. A hundred dollars."

"My car, too," I explained. "It's still on Wilshire, there. I'll get a ticket."

"There's no limit there. What are you trying to say, Joe?"

I smiled and climbed out of the car. "I guess I was trying to think of some chintzy way to say I was yellow. Let's go, tiger."

His smile was dim and doubtful. He hesitated a moment before walking along with me to the apartment building.

Kranyk came to the door. He looked at me without surprise and that verified my suspicion. I kept my hand in my pocket as we went in.

I looked around the mail-order decor and asked, "Where's your partner? Where's your sister?"

"She's not my sister, ginzo. Koski will be along in a minute." He looked at Harvest. "What did you tell him? How much?"

"Nothing," Harvest said.

I turned to look at the bland, cold face of Harvest. He met my stare and didn't change expression.

Kranyk said, "Koski will be here soon and we can talk all this out. You guys want a beer?"

Harvest shook his head. I said, "No, thanks."

And then I heard a familiar sound, the tappets on my Plymouth. I went quickly to the window, my hand still in my pocket. I pulled the drape to one side and saw my car pulling up in front. Koski was behind the wheel.

I turned back to see them both smiling at me. I smiled in return, and said to Harvest, "It's a good thing you had me phone Sergeant Macrae. These boys mean business, just as you told me they did."

Kranyk whirled and there was suddenly a gun in his hand and it was pointed at Harvest. "You double-crossing bastard," he said hoarsely.

Greg's face went slack and he said in near-hysteria, "He's trying to trick you, Eddie. Use your head. I brought him here, didn't I? He got smart too soon, that's all."

Now Kranyk turned back toward me, and the gun swung with him. But I had my own gun in my hand by this time and I let him have one right in the belly. He went slamming back, but he was still conscious, and I dropped to the floor as his shot went into the window behind me, showering glass.

He fell and Harvest ran toward the kitchen, and I went quickly to the front door and got to it just as it opened. Koski stood there, a gun half out of his pocket, and I said, "That's far enough."

I heard a sound behind me and turned quickly and saw Kranyk on the floor, the gun still in his hand and pointing at me. I dropped to the floor once more and the gun went off.

And Koski fell right across me, shot down by his buddy.

Women were screaming all over the building by this time, and from in front I could hear the Jag's sweet engine roaring and there was a squeal of tires as Gregory Harvest got the hell out of there.

I climbed out from under Koski and saw that this partner had finally lost consciousness. I went to the phone and asked the operator for the Venice Station and thanked my lucky stars that I was still alive.

And then from behind the oblivion came, a bull's-eye right smack on the top of my head. It must have been a vase, because one piece of pottery beat me to the floor.

And though I couldn't see her, I could recognize the nasal of the stocky blonde who was neither sister nor wife. She said shrillingly, "Damn you, I warned you not to mess up the place!"

Macrae chuckled and lighted a cigarette. He looked at the white square of bandage on top of my head and turned more serious.

"How are they?" I asked. "Did you get the report yet?"

"Kranyk will pull through. It's doubtful if Koski will. He's bleeding internally and they can't seem to stop it."

"I shot Kranyk. Kranyk shot Koski. Let's get that on the record right now."

"What difference does it make? You wouldn't go to the gas chamber for killing either one of them."

"It makes a difference to me," I answered. "I don't want to get a reputation as a killer."

He smiled. "Just a lady-killer, that's enough for you."

"How about Harvest?" I asked. "Was he picked up yet?"

Marcrae frowned and cleared his throat. "That's what I want to talk to you about. Your story is a little fishy there, Joe. Want to clean it up?"

It was uncomfortably quiet in the airless room. I said

angrily "Not *you!* Dumb you are, but not crooked. Just because Harvest is a buddy of the D.A.'s, is that it? Or does it go higher?"

He colored and half rose from his chair. "Puma, you're not that big. Nobody's that big. Take that back."

"When I hear your story, I'll take it back. The floor is yours, Sergeant Macrae."

He sat back in his chair again, his stare holding mine. "A man from the West Los Angeles station went directly to Harvest's office and he was there. And he claimed he'd never left with you. He claimed he'd told you he'd been threatened by Koski and Kranyk and you told him you'd go right over there to straighten it out."

"His word's better than mine? Because he's a big shot?"

Macrae shook his head. "Because his secretary corroborated every word of his statement. You left alone, she said. And another woman said the same thing. She was pulling up in front of the building, she claimed, when you left in your car, *alone.*"

"And what's her name?"

"Deborah Huntington," he said.

I said calmly, "Both women you mentioned have reason to lie and I know the reasons. If I were less of a gentlemen, I'd tell them to you. Right now, all I'm asking is your belief in me."

"After you called me a dumb crook?"

"I apologize. The reports aren't all in yet, Sergeant. There must have been half a dozen women screaming in Koski's apartment building and a couple of them must have seen that Jaguar gun out of there. Before you learn my story is true the hard way, why not accept it now, as one gentleman from another?"

He put his cigarette out slowly, starting at the ashtray. "Joe, for crying out loud, don't make a production out of it. Will you swear to me right now that you have *never* lied to a police officer, or withheld information from him?"

"If you'll swear to me that Harvest would still be getting this much courtesy if he wasn't a friend of the D.A.'s."

He looked up. "Easy, now."

"Easy, hell. I'm giving you a chance to be a whole man."

"I am a whole man. Or I'd be a lieutenant."

I said, "Harvest's secretary wasn't in the office when we left. And as for Miss Deborah Huntington, Harvest kept insisting to me that he was sure she had killed Duncan Guest."

"Oh? How come that's not in your report?"

"Because I thought it was nonsense."

"You let us decide what is nonsense and what isn't, Joe. We've given you a lot of leeway and we expect your full co-operation in return."

"Sergeant, you checked out Deborah Huntington. You checked her out thoroughly. Harvest was just making dialogue, trying to distract me from the real reason he sent for me."

"And the real reason . . . ?"

"Was to get me over to where those hoods could take care of me."

"And why would he want to do that? What threat were you to him or to them? Don't tell me they'd get that rough and that tricky just out of petulance."

"I can't think of any other reason. All three of them had reason to hate me, remember. I broke Harvest's hand and I located Koski and Kranyk for you."

"It doesn't add," he said. "It's too childish for pros."

"You're right," I said thoughtfully, "it doesn't." I stood up. "Am I free to go?"

"Of course," he said. He coughed. "But—ah—don't leave town."

"I—ah—won't," I said. "Thanks so much for all your faith in me, Sergeant."

"Don't mention it," he said.

FOURTEEN

HARVEST HAD GUTS; there was no doubting that. He had told the big lie, the daring, impossible lie, and it was temporarily being accepted. He couldn't do what would have been instinctive in his situation—he couldn't leave town. He had too much invested in his name and his practice here.

So he had told the daring lie, not the little one. And there was a possibility he was going to get away with it.

A prowl car took me to my car, still in front of the apartment building. The neighbors were all out on the lawns now, gassing and watching the front of the building, and I got a lot of attention from them, my new white bandage marking me as a participant.

A reporter from the *Mirror-News* caught me before I could get the Plymouth out of there and I was very polite to him, because the *Mirror-News* is owned by the *Times* and so is Los Angeles.

I gave the man a polite ten minutes and posed in three positions for the photographer he called over. I explained that I was working with the Department and had just about solved this double killing with some Department help.

I didn't tell him where I was going next, because I didn't think Arnold Giampolo had been behind the attack and I still owed him the silence I'd promised him.

I drove over to his place slowly, a throbbing in my head warning me that perhaps that vase had done more damage than the police physician had assumed.

A woman came to the door today, a fairly young woman who looked like a secretary, a well-paid secretary, a well-paid and agreeable secretary, a well-paid, agreeable and well-stacked secretary.

"My name is Joe Puma," I told her, "and it's very important that I see Mr. Giampolo right now."

"He's having lunch," she said doubtfully.

"Maybe we could all have it together," I said. "He promised me a meal a couple of days ago."

Her eyebrows lifted. "Joe Puma . . . ," she said thoughtfully. "I have a feeling the name should ring a bell."

"It's rung a lot of bells," I said. "Private investigator, bon vivant, romantic—just tell him the name, honey, and await his reaction."

"I know you now," she said. "This way, Mr. Puma."

I walked slowly behind her, keeping to a minimum the throbbing in my head. We walked through the living room, through the dining room, and into a paneled breakfast room that looked out onto the pool.

Arnold Giampolo was eating a thick soup. He looked up and saw the patch on my head. "What happened to you, Joe?"

I looked at the girl and back at him.

"You may go now, Daisy," he said. "Thank you."

She left, and he nodded toward a chair at the far end of the table from him. "Had lunch?"

"No."

"Have it with me."

"Thanks." I sat down. "Is her name really Daisy?"

He nodded and smiled. "Why?"

"Oh, Orchid or Camellia or even Rose. She simply doesn't look like a daisy."

His smile was forced. "Joe, Joe—a patch on your head and a gag on your lips. What happened to you?"

"I tangled with Koski and Kranyk," I said. "Kranyk will live but Koski might not. Neither one of them hurt me; it was that piano-legged blonde of Kranyk's who put the patch on my head."

He stared at me, his soup spoon halfway to his mouth. "Start at the beginning," he said, "and give it to me straight. Tell me everything, Joe."

I gave it to him straight, all of it. A maid brought me some of the soup, a creamy, rich mushroom soup and not canned. She brought me an omelette after that. I was eating fast and talking slow and finished with the airless room and my dialogue with Macrae just as we got to the coffee.

He took out a cigarette and I lighted it for him. He said, "San Francisco, eh? Harvest is making allies. He's a slick one, isn't he?"

"And together than he looks," I said.

Arnold Giampolo grimaced and held his breath for a moment. Then he said softly, "You don't think I was behind that trap, do you, Joe?"

"No," I said.

"Thank you. I wasn't. They've gone over to Harvest, the way it looks. You say Koski's in a bad way?"

"Sergeant Macrae told me it's doubtful if he'll pull through."

Again, some pain must have gripped him, for he grimaced and held his breath. "Could you wait a moment?" he said. "I need a little morphine."

"Of course," I said.

He left the room. My hand trembled as I lifted my coffee to my mouth. The lion was dying and the jackals

were closing in. Well, Mike Petalious would take care
of the jackals eventually, if he listened to someone
smarter, someone like his wife.

I was pouring another cup of coffee from the silver
pot when he came back in. He walked slowly and lightly,
like a man on eggs. He sat down again and smiled at
me dreamily.

"Great stuff," he said.

"I've heard it is. Mr. Giampolo, why me? What did
they want to get rid of me for? What kind of a threat
am I?"

"You're one of the few on your side of the fence who
knows Giampolo is king and Harvest crown prince.
You're the *only* man on your side of the law who knows
Petalious is the chosen heir. With you gone, that knowledge dies with you." He sipped his coffee. "Would you
like some cognac or something?"

"No, thank you. My head isn't quite right, yet."

He looked at me enviously. "Tough. Smart, sexy, tough
and active. Damn you, Joseph Puma."

I sipped the coffee and tried to smile at him. "I'm not
really smart, just windy."

"How would you like to be Mike Petalious' partner?
He needs somebody like you."

I shook my head. "I'm—fundamentally honest. I told
you I wasn't smart."

"Maybe it's not so stupid to be honest," he said.
"Maybe there are some rewards I've never considered."

"Honesty is a disease," I assured him. "And like most
diseases today, it's being exterminated slowly."

He licked his lips, nibbled them as though they itched.
"Why was Harvest trying to steer you onto Deborah
Huntington? What was his purpose there, do you think?"

"It was something to keep my mind off the obvious,
the obvious being that I was being led into a trap. He
had to have some excuse to get me to think he was
turning honest. Then, when the call came from Kranyk,
it would be logical for me to think you had sent that
pair against the honest Harvest. It all made sense until
I realized he had lied about the golf and this was all
so pat."

"You were lucky," he said.

"In a number of ways," I admitted. "I was lucky I

never had the tappets adjusted on my car, for one thing. And I was lucky I had broken Harvest's hand, or I wouldn't have known about the golf lie."

"Koski and Kranyk won't bother you any more," he promised. "I can't guarantee anything about Harvest. Now, about that psychiatrist, I know who he is. Curt Huntington asked me to recommend one and I recommended Doctor Light. I'll phone him for you, Joe."

"He wouldn't tell me anything, would he? Wouldn't it be a violation of his ethics?"

"Maybe. But I put him through medical school, so maybe he'd bend them a little for me, particularly if a murder is involved."

"I think it was just talk," I answered. "I doubt if there's a remote chance it would do me any good. She's too well covered. Even if she's the killer, she's too well covered to take into court."

"I'll phone him anyway," he said. "You can decide if you need him or not. And tell your Sergeant Macrae to hold both Koski and Kranyk if they recover. I'll send him enough to keep them in San Quentin for years."

I finished my coffee and stood up. "Well, thanks. I'm glad I kept you on my side with my silence."

As I went out, I heard him telling Daisy to get Doctor Light on the phone for him. He was dying with dignity, like a lion should, that much was evident. He was trying to leave everything clean behind him, reward his friends and avenge his enemies, like a man should.

The sun was out in full force and people were scurrying, worrying, breathing and conniving all over town. Loving, hating, eating and sleeping while the king took morphine to dull the biting pain.

I breathed deeply and walked slowly to the car. I didn't even hate Gregory Harvest at the moment but he had to be nailed to his home-made cross. That much I owed the dying lion.

In the outer office, his secretary looked at me fearfully. I nodded toward his door. "Judas in?"

She shook her head. "He's over at the West Side Station. He was picked up by two uniformed men about twenty minutes ago."

I sat in a chair next to her desk. "How wonderful. Why?"

"That—woman who hit you on the head said she saw him there at the apartment. And some other women there saw the Jaguar." She took a deep breath. "And then Miss Huntington—changed her story."

"Are they holding her, too?"

"No. She claims she saw your car leave and assumed you were driving it, but now she remembers the other man looked shorter than you are and she's sure it wasn't you."

"Fine. And how about you, Mrs. Schroeder? How come they didn't take you along? Or did you change your story, too?"

"I was out of the office," she said. "I didn't see either one of you leave."

"So they should have taken you along. Why didn't they? That isn't what you told them the first time."

She chewed her lower lip. "I called them—*before* they got any of the other stories. I told them my conscience was more important to me than my job."

"That's a good line," I said admiringly. "Did you give it a lot of emotional overtone?"

"You don't have to be sarcastic."

"Yes I do. May I use your phone?"

She nodded mutely, staring at me.

I phoned the Venice Station and Macrae was there. "What now?" he asked gruffly.

"An apology," I answered, "in the proper tone of voice."

"I'm sorry," he said in a near-falsetto. "I apologize for ever doubting you, Mr. Puma. I was a beast. *Drop dead!*"

I chuckled. "Now you'll never get beyond sergeant. See you later."

I hung up and looked thoughtfully at Mrs. Schroeder. "You don't, by chance, happen to have a cerulean mink stole, do you?"

She colored. "I don't even have a fox scarf. You have a nasty mind, don't you?"

"I meet so many nasty people," I explained. I stood up. "Give my regards to Mr. Schroeder. And remember that Gregory Harvest is not a man to forget a grievance. You still might not have made the smart move by phoning the police, Mrs. Schroeder."

"I wasn't trying to be smart," she said. "I was trying

to be honest. That's something you wouldn't understand."

I used a word I'd rather not repeat. It is a product of the bull. I left her with her mouth open and went out into the hot, late afternoon.

I hadn't been to my office all day and I sort of missed that drab little dump. I drove over there.

There was one check in the mail. It was a small check, but five months overdue and very welcome. There was a light bill and the bill for one of my insurance policies. I thought of Arnold Giampolo and made out a check for the insurance bill. My brother was my only heir but he could use the money; he was still going to college.

Deborah Huntington, killer. . . ? No. At one time, maybe, but she was a fairly reasonable woman now by feminine standards. All women are partially punchy; she wasn't much worse than the others.

My answering service informed me she had phoned at three o'clock. That was less than an hour ago.

Sheila Gallegan? Look at it objectively, Puma, not through the memory of last night. No.

Miss Quintana, soon to be Mrs. Mike Petalious? Maybe. I didn't know her very well. I had never slept with her. Damn it.

Ruth Schroeder?

The blonde with the football legs?

Mrs. Whitey Tullgren?

The model from Regal Furs? I never had followed through on her. Maybe I would, after the murder was solved.

Einar Hansen's sister?

Snip Caster's Aggie?

Nine women I had met and batted only .222. Figure it out for yourself, nine into two. That was pretty damned decent of me. My head throbbed and absurd and weird thoughts poured through it and I kept thinking of funerals. Why?

I went to the cooler and drank three paper cups full of water. I went to the washroom down the hall and bathed my face and neck in cool water. I had nothing to do. I had nowhere to go except to Doctor Light.

Show me the light, Doctor Light. A dizziness shook me as I straightened to dry my face and neck with paper towels. My face in the mirror above the sink looked pale and awry. It was not my face but my vision that was awry, I knew.

I had a small leather couch in my office, for emergencies, and I lay on that and tried to blank my mind. Was it a delayed reaction from the vase or too much thinking with a limited mentality?

Didn't I want to talk with Doctor Light? Didn't I want to know about Deborah? What was she to me except a spoiled, rich brat?

She was one of the girls I loved. I loved a lot of them and not only for the reasons you might be guessing. I love to talk with them, walk with them, eat with them, dance with them. They're much more interesting than men to me and always had been, long before I knew their ultimate gift.

I loved Deborah and Sheila, Miss Quintana and Mrs. Tullgren, the Regal Fur model and Ruth Schroeder and Daisy and even Aggie; I loved them all because they were women and this would be a sickening world without them.

The throbbing dimmed as the blood left my head and my vision was a little better. I got up and phoned Deborah.

"Returning your call," I explained. "Did you phone to hire me or fire me and what is my present status?"

"Let's not fight," she said quietly.

"You use that line a lot, Deb."

"Only with you. I'm sorry I told the police what I did. Even if I had thought that was you in the Plymouth, I shouldn't have told them anything like that."

"Why did you?"

"Because I started to come back to your place last night, about a half-hour after I'd left. And I saw Sheila Gallegan going up there. With an overnight bag."

"She was frightened," I explained. "Wouldn't you be, if you lived where she did, and lived alone, as she does?"

"*Please*, Joe. Don't make it worse by lying. Do all the frightened women in town spend the night at your place?"

"There isn't room. It's a small apartment. Do you know what your friend Greg Harvest was trying to sell me?"

"What?"

"The theory he supports, that you murdered Duncan Guest. He wanted to help me substantiate it."

"How?"

"We never got around to discussing that. People started shooting at me and I haven't seen him since."

"Are you free tonght?"

"Later, about eight, I will be."

"I still have the key. We won't fight, will we?"

"I won't. I hope you don't. I've a headache."

"I'll rub your forehead and sing lullabies," she promised. "Good-bye now."

I hung up and waited a few minutes before dialing the number I had been given. A woman answered, and I said, "This is Joseph Puma. Would it be possible for me to see Doctor Light before he goes home? Mr. Giampolo phoned him about me, this afternoon."

FIFTEEN

THE KEY WORD Doctor Light used was transvestitism and if you don't know what it is, you could look it up, as Mr. Thurber once said. It is latent in a lot of people, more often women than men, I would guess from a look around the world today. Particularly out here. It has led to some spectacular crimes, one recent example in the Middle West, in one of the dairy states. Under the milder drive, it is harmless and sells a lot of women's slacks.

It doesn't necessarily lead to lesbianism or homosexuality, but is quite often apparent in those afflictions.

That wasn't all he told me, but that was the trigger word and it revealed to me why the word *funeral* should have been bouncing around in my subconscious mind for so long.

People of decorum are likely to observe the social proprieties unless some strong repugnance prevents it. Right?

I had caught him at five-thirty, just before it was

time to go home, and spent half an hour with him and now I was hungry, despite the remnants of my headache. As long as I was in his office, I had asked him about the headache and he had assured me it was to be expected and unless it persisted tomorrow, further medical exploration would not be required.

I ate at Bar-B-Q Rancho and while I ate a Rancho Bar-B-Q, I thought about the earring. Earrings come in pairs, so far as I knew, and where was the other one?

If they were Sheila's earrings, why were they stolen in the first place? The killer, if my theory was correct, had enough money to buy better earrings than those. Once stolen, of course, the earring in Einar Hansen's hand was an effective red herring, temporarily effective, at least. And in Sergeant Macrae's mind Sheila Gallegan still had a lot of explaining to do about the one in Einar Hansen's hand.

But why were they taken in the first place?

Add it up, Puma, all that is obvious, the lies and the attitudes and the conflicting statements of the participants and the bystanders and try to see why a pair of ordinary seventeen-dollar earrings were stolen.

Perhaps the killer thought they were more valuable than that? Even if they were, what difference would it make?

Did the killer know they were Sheila's?

Sheila knew they were Sheila's.

According to my theory, Sheila was not the killer.

So go back: did the killer know they were Sheila's?

It hit me, then, an interesting and highly plausible theory, and I went to the phone booth next to the cashier's desk.

I called the Venice Station, but Macrae had gone home. I told them it was important and they gave me his home phone number.

I told him, "I've got a pretty strong hunch and I want some people rechecked, some neighbors and friends."

"Let's hear the hunch, first."

"No," I said. "You've got to ride with me, Sergeant. This would require some shenanigans I'm sure no police officer would want to be a part of."

"Sure. And the three grand is yours, too, huh?"

"Goodness me," I said in surprise, "hasn't that offer of Devine's been withdrawn?"

"Don't get cute," he said. "You haven't the build for it. We pussyfoot around, getting the case strong enough for trial, and you confront the killer and get three grand."

"Sergeant," I said nobly, "five hundred of it to the Pension Fund when and if I collect."

"Okay."

"Providing," I added, "that when you get a confession, if any, Devine is notified so he can have his picture taken at the station. Maybe for that kind of publicity, I could even milk another five hundred out of him for the Pension Fund."

"Lord, you're a cynical man. Okay."

"How about Harvest?" I asked. "Got a case?"

"God knows. He is a slippery one and one hell of a lawyer. And the influential friends that man has got—"

"He's got a broken hand," I said consolingly, "and I have a strong feeling that he'll have more than that if he ever tangles with a certain man who has reason to hate him."

"What certain man? What are you witholding, Puma?"

"Only what I must, Sergeant. Only enough to keep me functioning and solvent. Our only cooperative concern is murder; let's stick with that." I took a breath. "How about Koski and Kranyk?"

"Koski died. That will take care of Kranyk."

"He didn't mean to shoot his buddy."

"Ain't that too damned bad? Are you crying for him?"

"You're a cynical man, Sergeant. Check these people now, the same neighbors you checked before and the same servants."

It was now seven o'clock and I drove home. My headache was almost gone but I didn't feel well, by any means. I got home at seven-twenty and took a hot and soapy shower and my aches went away and some of my tensions. I had some things to explain carefully and delicately and perhaps they could be explained better in bed. I added a touch of the manly cologne a client had given me.

She came before eight, bringing another bottle of Jack Daniels. Or maybe it was the same bottle, for all I knew. She said, "You look worried. Bad day?"

"Bad day. What's my attraction, Deb?"

"To me? Or to Sheila Gallegan?"

I said nothing, waiting patiently.

"You're—both gentle and virile," she finally answered. "That isn't a very common combination in men." She kicked off her shoes. "And of course you're always—available. Would *insatiable* be a better word?"

I didn't answer.

"No more questions?" she asked mockingly. "Do you have a cigarette handy?"

I reached into the pocket of my terry-cloth bathrobe and brought out a cigarette. I lighted it for her and said, "You're a big girl now, aren't you? Ready to face the world and the facts?"

She nodded. She unbuttoned the top three buttons of her blouse.

I asked, "Do you have a pair of jet pendant earings?"

She took a deep breath and stared at me.

"You're a big girl now," I reminded her. "Do you have a pair of jet pendant earings?"

She nodded gravely. "You know everything now, don't you?"

I shrugged. "Curt should have gone to the funeral. A man of his decorum is expected to observe the proprieties. Particularly after he made such a great public show of being a friend and admirer of Duncan Guest's. Curt hated Duncan Guest, didn't he?"

She nodded solemnly. She put the cigarette carefully on an ashtry and bent over to peel off her stockings.

"Einar knew he hated him, because Einar was close to Guest. He knew Guest was despicable in Curt's eyes. That's what gave Einar his lead." I paused. "And caused his death."

She looked up to stare at me, the fragile stockings still in her hand. She put them silently and timidly on a chair.

"And," I went on, "Curt feels protective toward you, whether you know it or not. And he must have known what a degraded, double-gaited piece of scum this Duncan Guest was. The night he killed him, he saw those earrings in Guest's apartment and thought they were yours. He certainly didn't want the police to find them there and trace them to you. So he took them along. Later, when he learned they weren't yours, he used one of them as a red herring on Einar Hansen. Because if the police thought a woman had killed Guest, an earring in the hand of Einar Hansen might lead them to think the same woman killed Hansen."

Deborah didn't look surprised, only shocked and sad. She unbuttoned the rest of her blouse and hung it neatly on the chair. She said quietly, "I'm sure Curt didn't know they were Sheila's earrings."

"I'm sure he didn't. When did you—first learn he was a transvestite?"

She took a deep breath. "A few years ago. I was out one night, walking along the path above the house there. And one of the drapes in Curt's bedroom was partially open." She looked at the floor. "I saw him in a black chiffon dress, wearing a wig. Later, when he was away on a trip, I went through his bedroom for half a day before I found this secret closet."

"Does he know you know?"

She shook her head, fumbling with the stuck zipper on her skirt. "I doubt it."

"Is that when you started going to the psychiatrist?"

She nodded.

"Did you suspect all along he was the murderer?"

She looked up from the stuck zipper to face me candidly. "I had such a small suspicion, my rational mind told me it was absurd. But I had to know. I'm a big girl now, and I *have to know.*"

"Didn't the police check him for that night?"

She nodded. "And Greg Harvest was his alibi. As a matter of fact, when Greg swore he was with him at the time, I thought I might have been wrong."

"Greg lied for him? Then Greg must have known."

She said musingly, "Who can tell what Greg Harvest knows or doesn't know? He's a strange man." She straightened, once more ignoring the zipper. "Tell me honestly, now, do the police have to know?"

I gave it some thought, or pretended to. I didn't want her to think I was callous. While I pretended to think, she went back to the zipper and conquered it. She put the skirt carefully on the same chair that held her other clothes.

She stood there quietly in white lace panties and wired bra, studying me, and waiting for my answer.

"The police have to know," I said finally. "Einar Hansen and Guest weren't much. But in their unique ways, they were human beings. So Curt's fate is not ours to judge, it's the law's, and if we are mature, we support the law. Can you understand that, Deb?"

"I can understand that," she said.

"Anything I can do to keep it quiet as possible, I will do," I promised her. "We'll keep the newspapers toned down. You know I'll do anything I can for you, don't you, Deborah?"

"I know you will," she said. She turned around. "And you can start by unhooking my bra."

We were back in the airless room, Macrae and I. Adonis was in another room with his body make-up on, having his picture taken in a number of poses, holding the check in all of them.

I said, "You picked up Huntington. Have you got Harvest, too?"

"And how. Right where the hair is short. We've got that man in a knot at the moment. He doesn't know whether to spit or go blind. He can't be sure right now where his best interests lie."

"Once he learns," I said, "that's the way he'll go. How about Curtis Huntington?"

Macrae shook his head wonderingly. "Damnedest thing, I think he's worried more about his sister's reputation than his own neck. He claims that angle about the trasver—what the hell is that word?"

"Transvestitism," I answered. "It means an urge to wear the clothes of the opposite sex. Like women in riding habits and men in silk Hawaiian sport shirts."

"Well, this went a little further than that, huh?"

"Yes. What's his complaint?"

"It will look freakish, he claims," said Macrae. "That won't bother him, where he is likely to be, but it will reflect on his sister and he won't confess unless we promise to keep that angle from the newspapers."

"Promise him," I said. "It will protect his sister and get the confession from him. And consider, Sergeant, where the confession from him will put Harvest, lying to a police officer."

"Yes," he said. "Ah, yes." He smacked his lips.

"And maybe he'd throw in a little donation to the Pension Fund," I pointed out cynically.

"Watch your tongue," he said harshly. "That would be crooked."

"Huh!" I said.

"And exactly what does that mean?"

"It's your word. You threw it at me; I'm now throwing it back. Huh!"

A uniformed man came in and said, "Harvest wants to deal. How about it? Detective Levine asked me to ask you."

"I'll answer for the Sergeant," I told the officer. "The answer is *huh!* Right, Sergeant?"

Macrae nodded. "But I want to talk with Huntington. Joe, here, thinks we should protect his sister's name as much as possible, and we have reason to humor Joe. I think we can permit Mr. Huntington a few—minor graces."

"Because of the Pension Fund," I explained to the officer.

His face lighted up and he looked at Macrae. "Is he going to do it, Sergeant?"

Macrae colored. There was a silence. The officer suddenly looked uncomfortable. For the first time since I'd met him, Macrae actually looked embarrassed.

He said gruffly to the officer, "You may go. Beat it!"

The officer went out and Macrae looked at the top of his desk.

"Something is rotten in Venice," I said quietly. "Confess, oh invulnerable one. Something has happened to shame you in front of me."

He looked at me rigidly.

"It's about the Pension Fund," I said. "This sea of red faces started when that officer asked if I was going to do it. Do what, man of impeccable integrity?"

"We'll keep her name out of it, Joe," he said softly. "Because you want us to, Miss Huntington's name will stay spotless."

"And for this," I asked cynically, "what does Joe Puma do?"

Some of his blush was gone but his voice was timid. "Well, this idea of Devine contributing to the Pension Fund was your idea, not mine. I didn't even voice it to Devine."

"One of your lackeys did," I said, "or Devine wouldn't be down here, drowned in flash bulbs. Carry on, Sergeant."

Macrae took a deep breath. "Devine heard about your

fight with Petalious. It's some kind of an obsession with him, the way he feels about Petalious, isn't it?"

"Yes. Mike broke his arm, once."

"Some time ago. Devine thinks he's better now. He's almost pathological about how much better he is. If you'll go against him, he says, he'll contribute five hundred to the Pension Fund, just for trying him out, Joe. And in the one-in-a-million chance that you might win, he'll up his donation to *one thousand dollars*."

I smiled, enjoying the discomfiture of dour Sergeant Macrae. I said. "Devine isn't better than he was; he's worse. Ever since he left college and got into the fraudulent end of this game, he's got into bad habits. Real wrestlers never leave their feet, Sergeant. They don't have these flying blocks or tackles, these running head butts. They stay solid and use their leverage and their skill. This Devine is off his feet too much and that would make him vulnerable."

"How, Joe?"

"The same way a bull is. That's all he is, a golden-headed bull."

Macrae said hopefully. "It would be quite a test, a bull against a stud. It would be interesting to watch."

"I wouldn't be a stud against Devine," I said. "I'd be a bull fighter. We adjust to the ground and the enemy, Sergeant. But there is no ground to defend, is there? This is a pipe dream. Where would we fight?"

Macrae looked past me, hope now stronger than the embarrassment in his face. "The boys thought we could use the pistol range. It's well lighted." He coughed. "After the reporters have gone, of course."

"Of course," I said, "or you'd be back to driving a truck for a living. Most of those pistol ranges are well timbered, pretty solid. How about this one?"

"Two walls of solid four-by-fours, Joe. You'll do it?"

"For Deborah Huntington and the Pension Fund," I said profoundly, "for a theory I have about the idiocy to which a great college sport has been degraded and for the continuance of the myth and legend of Joe Puma, I will do this."

"After the reporters have gone, of course," he said.

"Of course, Sergeant," I said gently.

The lights were good and two of the walls were thick. One of the other walls filled with baled straw and the wall where the shooters stood was occupied by a waist-high counter.

Adonis wore his wrestling tights. I had taken off my shoes and jacket and shirt. He smiled confidently at me and around at the half dozen officers who stood behind the counter. He was confident he had learned all the tricks since leaving college. He had learned the tricks, I was sure, but he had forgotten how to wrestle. The tricks were not wrestling tricks, they were theatrical tricks designed to titillate an ignorant audience.

He seemed bathed in a golden glow, his muscle bulging, his light hair a halo, his arms swinging freely and eagerly. Catch as catch can and I would be permitted to do everything but bite and scratch.

Somebody hit a pan, and he came for me, lightly, carefully, his eyes on my face but missing nothing. I thought of the night he cried and hoped I could once again bring him to that adolescent emotional state. My best hope was to frustrate him enough to make him wild, to bring him to the moment of truth I planned for him.

When he was four feet away, still out of the reach of an arm, he paused, and I feinted, pretending to go around him to the right.

He rushed and he rushed toward the way I feinted. I stepped quickly to the left as he rushed and I kept my ring hand rigid and open as I chopped down savagely as the back of his neck.

It was no neck, it was a muscled pillar of steel, and my hand bounced off harmlessly and I tried to spin with him, but he had turned quickly and he had my right hand in his, and he swung me.

He threw me, all two hundred and twenty pounds of me, and I rolled on the hard floor and as I reached my back, I saw him dive.

That could have been the end, right here. But my knee went up automatically and it caught him in the groin as he dove, and he grunted and fell to the right, reaching for my arm again.

I didn't let him have the arm, but I gave him the

hand. I gave it to him balled into a fist and I gave it to him in the teeth. I felt a tooth go and his cry was hoarse as I tried to scramble to my feet.

He must have been wearing a cup or that knee would have taken his strength. It hadn't taken any strength. His big hand had my ankle before I could completely gain my feet, and I went sprawling and he scampered along the floor with one fist raised.

I moved my head enough to miss the full fury of the blow, but it caught me on the cheek and the cheek-bone was chipped, I felt sure. I didn't try to look good; my strategy had gone awry, and I threw my left hand out wildly to ward him off as I rolled for clearance in undignified retreat.

He came scrambling after me as our audience watched, silent as mutes. This was no wrestling audience and I hoped it wouldn't make Adonis realize different tactics must be employed in a match of this kind, away from the television cameras.

I prayed that the ham in him would remain constant. I needed his need for the theatrical.

As he scrambled after me now, he reached, and as he reached I kicked and my bare foot caught him in the shoulder. It slowed him only enough for me to get to my feet, but that was all I wanted. That was where I had to be to get back to my strategy on this one.

I was on my feet and he got to his. Blood dripped down from one corner of his mouth, and he paused, studying me, balanced evenly on his feet, ready to move either way.

In his eyes I thought I saw the first faint glimmering of doubt, and I hoped I could fan it to the madness of frustration. The wall was behind me now, and I could guess he was waiting to see which way I'd move, so he could pin me against something solid.

I moved the way he probably hadn't anticipated; I moved straight for him, and I brought a hook along. There was no point in trying to hit him in the belly; that, like his neck, was corded steel. Boxers are hard there, but a boxer can't possibly afford the muscle development of a wrestler or he would never be able to move around a ring.

So I hooked the left high, toward the jaw, and it missed. But he had moved his head to avoid it, and my right hand caught him close enough to the button to stagger him.

I didn't go in after that. I had a different strategy. I could hit him hard enough to put him down, perhaps, but the finish was to be by wrestling rules. He would need to be flat on his back for that and not able to squirm a shoulder free, which would stop the count.

So I jabbed him off balance and moved away. I stepped in again, and slapped him sharply with the flat of my right hand and the dullness in his eyes went away and a gleam came back and I was hoping he would remember his night of ignominy under the hands of Mike Petalious.

I think he did. He rushed, both hands reaching, his vision imperfect and his intent dishonorable. He muttered something as he rushed, and I moved lightly to one side and stuck a foot out.

He stumbled to his knees and stayed there for seconds, shaking his head for clarity, on all fours. If he had pawed the floor, the symbolism would have been complete. The golden bull was summoning his strength and his cunning.

"Drop on him," Macrae called. "Now's the time, Joe."

I shook my head. My strategy was sounder, I felt. With both of us on the floor, the advantage would be his. That much he must have remembered from college.

He rose slowly and I had a moment of indiscretion, looking at the dulled hate in his eyes. I moved in.

He moved fast, faster than I thought he presently could, and he had the arm again, and started to swing. This time I took a chance, and fought his momentum, coming in, my head high.

He saw that expanse of open neck and the lure was too much. He let go of my arm and reached for the neck as I brought my head down sharply into his face.

This time he shouted shrilly and one hand went to his battered nose as I stepped quickly free, backing away from him, my hands up.

He rushed to my right; I moved to my left. He rushed to my left, I moved to my right. If I had held a cape, I couldn't have worked him much better. I didn't need

a cape and I wouldn't be permitted a sword. I taunted
him quietly: "Charge, Toro, charge. Come and get me,
muscle man, break me with your big hands."

He paused, a sight to see, his face bloody, his nose
awry, his eyes holding nothing human at the moment.

He charged and I moved away, toward the wall.

He turned and put his head down and charged again,
and his shoulder scraped my hip, throwing me momentarily off balance, and he turned quickly, his head
lowered, his eyes watching my feet, knowing where
they went, I had to go, knowing that if he could center
on my belly, that battering-ram of a head on top of
that massive neck would fold me like an accordion. At
least, it had always worked that way in front of the
television cameras.

There was another pause, two seconds before the
moment of truth, while his eyes watched my feet, his
arms went out to his sides and he shrugged his big
shoulders.

This time he came faster than he had in even that
first second of the fight, much faster than I had thought
he could ever move. I saw that hard head approaching
and was frightened for the first time, because it was
so damned close and coming so damned fast.

But I made it, though I felt the wind of his body
hurtling past. I stepped clear and put my right hand
on his rump, adding that needed dash of impetus to
his blind and raging charge.

His head went into those four-by-fours with a sickening
thunk and even from the calloused audience behind the
counter, there was a sigh of horror.

For anyone but a wrestler, that would have been the
end. But those absurd neck muscles had withstood the
shock, and he went down, but he wasn't out.

I went in with my five-fingered sword. He was trying
to get up, and I helped him. I swung him away from
the wall and brought up the right hand from my knees,
trying to drive the fist all the way through to the back
of his neck. It's all in the follow through, you must
remember, it's all in the follow through.

They could have counted to a hundred.

I took a shower right there. There wasn't any point in hurrying home. Deborah must have been asleep by now. And if she wasn't, there was still that bottle of Jack Daniel's we hadn't opened.

She was a big girl now, but I owed her the solace of that, just for tonight.

THE END
of a Crest Novel of Suspense by
William Campbell Gault

Printed in the United States
By Bookmasters